T0208615

Sunrise Mystique

A.T. Hartley

iUniverse, Inc.
New York   Bloomington

Sunrise Mystique

iUniverse books may be ordered through booksellers or by contacting:

*iUniverse
1663 Liberty Drive
Bloomington, IN 47403
www.iuniverse.com
1-800-Authors (1-800-288-4677)*

*Because of the dynamic nature of the Internet, any Web addresses or
links contained in this book may have changed since publication and may
no longer be valid. The views expressed in this work are solely those of
the author and do not necessarily reflect the views of the publisher, and
the publisher hereby disclaims any responsibility for them.*

*ISBN: 978-1-4401-6584-9 (pbk)
ISBN: 978-1-4401-6583-2 (ebook)*

Printed in the United States of America

iUniverse rev. date: 09/10/2009

Chapter 1

"But, Mom, you promised!" Becky cried. "You said you'd be here with me, THIS TIME."

"I'm telling you this is *really important.* We'll get together and burn some serious plastic when I get back. Why don't you go shopping with some of your school friends or go out to dinner on me? Gotta go, Rebecca. Have loads to do before the limo picks me up. The corporate jet leaves soon." Not waiting for her daughter's reply, "Ta, Ta," she said and then the phone went dead.

Rebecca Allison Wells sat on her Victorian style canopy-bed, in a mauve silk nightgown, deep in thought. Her spacious bedroom was connected to a sitting room having a huge picture window in the exclusive North Chicago high-rise. The window framed a breath-taking panoramic view of the Lake Michigan shoreline and the metropolitan Chicago skyline to the south. Her suite of rooms was professionally decorated, looking like a feature article in a lady's interior design magazine, elegant, but lacking warmth. The calendar on her Queen Ann desk announced December 26, 1992. Her eighteenth birthday had come and gone two days ago, as silently as the dead of night. The weather was frigid and gloomy, "Another *miserable* Chicago winter," Becky groaned.

She looked at the large mirror on her collector's edition vanity. The young woman staring back at her was a contradiction. She knew her size. She was five feet zero, weighing a hundred pounds, waist-length dark brown hair, and vibrant blue eyes. She was a cheerleader at her exclusively private all girl high school that gave her athletically feminine muscles covering her 36-22-32 petite frame.

"Why are you crying?" the girl in the mirror asked sympathetically.

Becky looked back angrily, "As if you didn't know," she spat. Becky had talked to herself, since she was a little girl. As an only child, she spent most of her time away from school alone and she didn't get along with the other girls in class. To them she was a haughty little biach who had everything. Her evil witch mother performed amazing tricks with the wave of her powerful wand. Becky called her imaginary friend Cathy, after the little girl who lived next door to her grandparents, who kindly let Becky play with Cathy as a child. Becky's mother didn't let her play with common people. Common people were mere mortals.

And so started her argument with Cathy, her reasonable self. Cathy was different than Becky. Becky wanted to love, to be free and to experience life in all its color. Cathy was so - levelheaded, the practical girl her mother adored.

Cathy fired the opening volley, "Just look at your closet, Becky. You have all the designer fashions a teenage girl could dream of. Why the tears?"

Tears streamed down Becky's cheeks. It was going to be a good cry this time she felt as she screamed back, "Yes! Yes, mother buys me everything a credit card can buy, but I can't buy my mother's love! That's all I want, Cathy, is love. Is that such a sin? I want a gentle hug, a soft brush of my hair, a tender kiss, and a family to enjoy on holidays. Is that too much to ask for? Is it?"

Becky and Cathy glared at each other angrily in the mirror. Becky wasn't going to back down today. Her mother had crossed the line. She'd purposely stayed away from my birthday two days ago and conveniently had a series of business meetings in Geneva over my Christmas through New Years holidays.

"And I got to spend my two special days of the year alone, AGAIN," Becky wailed. "It was you and I for Christmas dinner. Yes of course there was the maid and the female cook, but they don't count. Oh, what a rousing crowd we had!"

Cathy was hurt over the last comment, but she struggled for a comeback. She looked around the aristocratic apartment. It was hollow, having the feeling one gets at a mortuary, elegant but eerie.

Becky sensed she'd hurt her friend, the imaginary little girl she hadn't seen, in reality, for over fourteen years. "I'm sorry Cathy that I hurt your feelings. You're my best friend, but I want more Cath. I want to love, to feel warm air blow through my hair, to feel the sun on my skin, the excitement of a beautiful party, not the contrived social scene mother has planned for me, to attend all the right schools, to know the right people ... Is it wrong to want to be held by a handsome gentle-bred young hunk as we waltz in the moonlight?" Becky held out her open empty arms imagining.

"I know mother gives me every material gift imaginable, but that's not what I want." she blinked after a moment. "What I want most from mother isn't here. Somewhere in mother's rise to unimaginable power as head of her international bank and an attorney in corporate law, she's forgotten how to love."

Becky smoothed her satin sheets. She confessed to Cathy, "Over the last year I've tried to talk to mother about the things that are bothering me. Things I want. I had to call her secretary to make appointments. I felt like I'm scheduling appointments with a psychologist, not my mother, but I did it. I tried to explain to her that love was very important to me. She doesn't understand love. You can see that with her and Dad! Dad was a once successful real estate magnet from an influential New England family. Then mother destroyed his self-esteem. She cut him off from her love. Soon he found love with his male friend, and then mother divorced him. In one of our nasty arguments, she let it slip that I was A MISTAKE. That I caused her to miss her first big chance of success in life."

Becky took a slow breath; "Things haven't changed,

3

because mother doesn't want it different. She's happy the way things are, but I'm not! Mother and I speak two different languages. I'm young, full of life, a romantic. She's middle-aged, a yuppie, and so fake."

Becky sighed, "I've made up my mind Cathy, I'm leaving. You can come with me or stay. It's up to you."

There! It was said. The glove tossed down in challenge.

Cathy knew she wasn't going to change Becky's mind. She was right. Her mother had crossed the line this time, "If you're going, I can't stop you any more. I'll come along, just to see how things will turn out," she harrumphed.

Becky got out of bed and quickly dressed. Today was Saturday. She picked up her prepacked, school backpack, as if she were going to go to a classmate's house to study, and picked up her carefully hoarded cash. Over the last year, she'd saved over two thousand dollars. This was difficult, because she wasn't given cash. Her mother gave her own gold credit card on her thirteenth birthday as a present. All of her purchases were gladly covered without question but cash, was an easily identified deviation. She learned that her mother carefully checked her credit card bill, to see what Becky did, where she went.

She rode the elevator down to the ground floor and left the apartment building. The doorman didn't think anything unusual, since this was, how she often left for school or shopping trips. The only difference today was that instead of requesting the contracted limousine service, she walked down the street, turned the corner, and secretly got on a public bus for downtown.

In center-city Chicago, she noticed the stares she received over her abundant figure and expensive clothes. She walked to the central bus terminal and went into the ladies' room. Here she began her transformation. Here she left her unhappy world behind.

Her mother never let Becky leave their apartment building

except in elegant clothes or professionally coordinated outfits. Today would be different. Today she'd join the world around her.

Inside one of the stalls, Becky changed into a wash-worn flannel shirt, an oversized navy blue t-shirt, and jeans; she had swapped with one of her school classmates. She cut off most of her long brown hair with a pair of sewing sheers and put her hank of hair in a trash can. She stuffed her expensive fir lined coat and tweed skirt with a jacket suit into her backpack and put it in a different trash can inside the ladies' room.

She then left, looking very different from when she entered, careful to not look up in case security cameras were watching. She walked to the terminal beauty salon to get her hair trimmed. She hoped to appear like a longhaired boy in loose fitting clothes. With her disguise complete she walked to the Greyhund ticket counter and bought her pass to freedom.

She had thought long and hard about this part of her escape. She had no doubt when she didn't show up for school on Monday, her mother would have an army of private investigators hard on her trail. Her mother kept a PI firm on retainer to uncover all sorts of dirt on her business adversaries. Becky was determined to elude her trailing bloodhounds and carefully cover her tracks.

Becky had lived her whole life near Lake Michigan, which was cold most of the year. The frigid chill was too much like her life. Now was her chance to change all that. She wanted to add some warmth to her life and heart, but where to go in late December? For starters, she knew she at least liked water.

She bought herself several magazines and a newspaper. Next she went to the cafeteria and had a quick dinner before boarding the bus. Within two hours after buying her ticket, Becky was on a five-star cruiser on a non-stop run from Chicago. She knew she needed to put distance between herself and the windy city, so she did just that.

Her bus headed south. By mid-afternoon, she rolled

through St. Louis, then southern Missouri, down the entire length of Arkansas, along the eastern side of Louisiana.

On the bus, Becky stared out the window. Cathy took this chance to talk to Becky, "It would be nice to go to Grandma and Grandpa's house again," she hinted.

Becky signed, "Yes and no," she answered Cathy, her imaginary friend.

"I don't understand," Cathy questioned. "Your grandparents, George and Marta Wolefski were the sweetest people I knew. George was a union plumber and Marta was a housewife, they lived all their lives in Scranton Pa, being married when Marta was 18 and George was 21. They were married for 53 happy years. They lived a very simple life but were pleased, they owned their row home in the Polish part of town, close to friends and family in the parish."

Becky relaxed for the first time since running away as she chatted with Cathy, "Oh, how I loved grandma and grandpa's life," Becky remembered, "it was so predictable. Grandpa left the house for work at 7:30 am each weekday to return home precisely at 5 pm each weeknight. Grandma would dutifully have dinner warm and on the table when grandpa came through the door."

"I loved the summer your mother let you come visit your grandparents," Cathy recalled all those years ago, but admitted, "even though it probably was, so she could save on your expensive daycare over the summer."

Becky thought with a smile, "I loved Grandma and Grandpa's weekly menu, on Monday's, they had meatloaf, on Tuesday's, they had pork chops, on Wednesday's had kielbasa and kraut, on Thursday's, they had leftovers, and on Friday's of course fish. Oh gosh I remember grandma and grandpa drinking their coffee from jelly jars, unless company would come over. They both prepared their coffee adding cream from a condensed milk can that sat on the table and added sugar from a cereal bowl. They were humble, but honest people. I miss them so. They both passed away last year, six months apart from each other, and I'll never see them again," Becky moaned tearfully.

Cathy grinned, trying to lighten the somber mood, "I always loved Saturdays at the Polish-American Club. That's where I first met you."

Becky rebounded; she couldn't help herself, "Oh, that was the highlight of the week for all of us." Becky remembered. "Precisely at 4 PM every Saturday afternoon, grandpa started up the car and waited for grandma and I to come out of the house. Then he held the door for grandma and I to get in the car in our dresses. Other than for church, that was the only time I saw grandpa wear a coat and tie. Once at the club, grandpa joined the men having a mug of beer and grandma and I joined the other women, sipping tea. I loved how the women enjoyed being women, proud of who, and what they were, very basic but proud. Then we went in and had dinner. Grandpa bought food for us, anything on the menu. After dinner, there were more drinks and of course there was dancing."

Cathy asked gently, "Becky, we can turn around and go home."

Becky's face soured, "We've had this discussion, Cathy. My minds made up. If this is how you're going to be, then keep quiet," she fumed.

Cathy did as she was told. She faded into the shadows silently.

In the dark of night, the bus pulled into the downtown bus station in New Orleans. Here Becky put the second part of her plan into action, she bought a newspaper, a baseball hat, and walked around a bit.

She didn't want to make it easy for the private investigators that would certainly soon be on her trail. Traveling by bus and paying for her tickets in cash, made it near impossible to trace her, since there was no record of her name. She walked over to the Trailweys ticket counter and bought another pass. Within an hour, she was out on the Interstate. Biloxi Mississippi quickly passed behind her, as did Mobile, Alabama. She fell asleep as her freedom-machine headed east, then changed to a northeast direction.

Once again, in the dark of night, careful never to look up, Becky arrived in the Atlanta metro bus station and added a little spice to her escape. By traveling to major cities, she added thousands of possibilities to her escape, making her getaway hopefully untraceable.

She liked water, but she wasn't sure which way to go along the Atlantic seashore. Taking a quarter from her pocket, she trusted her fate to chance and tossed the coin to make her decision. Heads - south and to Florida, tails – northeast to the Carolinas. Lady Luck spoke and heads it was. Becky this time went to the Academic Bus Line counter, paying cash, and bought another ticket. By six AM on the next day, she got off the bus into the warm, moist air of Miami.

She had slept quite a bit on the buses, knowing that this part of her escape would be ticklish. She stored her backpack in a locker and then found the terminal's cafeteria. The breakfast crowd was quickly consuming large plates of food as she slid onto a stool at the end of the counter of the 50s style dinner.

Waitresses scurried about, rushing hot breakfasts to patrons' eager to begin their day, to catch a bus, or get to a job. A harried looking, a middle-aged woman with a wisp of graying hair that strayed from her pony-tail, in a classic waitress outfit with frilled apron quickly turned over the coffee cup in front of Becky and filled it with steaming black coffee. A dish of cream cups followed. The frazzled waitress looked at the new customer at her end of the counter and promised, "I'll be right back for your order in a minute." Becky looked at the embroidered name on her uniform-dress and mumbled, "No hurry, Blanche. I'm not in any rush." This caught the waitress's notice, but she was thankful.

At first Blanche wasn't sure if her new customer was a boy or a girl. This stranger was dressed in faded loose fitting clothes and longish brown hair under a baseball cap careful not to look up. Blanche had trouble telling sexes these days, but when her young customer had answered not to hurry, she heard a slightly high tone that hinted at the newcomer might be a girl. This got Blanche to thinking as she rushed orders to customers who were on a schedule. It had been a long, nonstop morning and her tired feet were screaming. She had started work at four am, and it was almost nine am before she got a chance to rest.

Blanche kept her mystery customer's coffee cup filled as was the policy of the dinner (buy the first cup and refills are free) while the customer read the morning's newspaper. She noticed that her customer seemed to concentrate on the classified section. Once when her young customer reached out for a sugar dispenser at the next stool, the loose fitting navy-blue T-shirt pulled taunt for a brief moment over a large roundness on the stranger's chest. Blanche smiled to herself, her first impression was right. No boy had a chest like that. Blanche started to slow down as the morning rush ebbed and a kinship started to develop between she and her young patron sitting at the far end of the counter.

Finally, Blanche's other customers left, and she could sit down. Her chair behind the counter was within arm's length of the mystery girl. Blanche refilled the quiet-one's cup and poured some coffee for herself. As Blanche stirred in some sugar, she started what she knew would mostly be a one-way conversation, "Just off the bus?" she half-asked, half-stated.

The flannel shirted patron simply nodded her head yes as she put her paper to the side and took up her freshly refilled cup. Blanche smiled as she lit a cigarette, "You remind me of myself, twenty-three years ago." The newcomer's eyebrows rose. Blanche noticed that her customer wasn't wearing any makeup, but from the professionally sculptured eyebrows on her young friend, this stranger came from a well-to-do family. Blanche laughed with a wise, good-natured laugh as she exhaled a cloud of smoke.

"Yeah, now that I think of it, it was twenty-three years ago in that same seat, doing about the same things you're doing now. I was fresh off the bus myself, fresh from my parent's farm back in Iowa. I was tired of the cold and unhappy where I was. I figured I could do better on my own. Over the years, I've seen a few girls make it, but I've also seen a world of heartache too."

Blanche took another drag on her cigarette and a sip of coffee, "Can I get you to go back honey? You know you could go back home and the folks won't be too mad that you missed a few days of school?"

The newcomer was quiet for a few moments as she put her cup back in the saucer and calmly asked, "Am I that easy to read?" This time it was Blanche's turn to raise her eyebrows as the young customer quietly, but stone cold said, "I've got nothing back home, and no one to go home to."

Blanche had seen this before. She didn't really believe the girl's story. She was too well kept to claim no family, but she wouldn't argue what the girl said. Blanche had been the same way. She leaned back in her chair and rubbed her sore calf muscles as she scrunched up her nose in resignation and thought, 'Yeah, I'm not getting any younger, but Maria, had been there for me,' Blanche thought. 'This girl looked clean and drug-free. Her eyes were clear and sharp.'

"Years ago," Blanche went on, "as I said, I sat in the same spot you're in now, in more ways than one. Lucky for me though, there was a waitress working the morning I blew into town; who turned out to be my patron saint. She kept me from disaster. You know Miami is a rough town?" Becky blinked. She hadn't thought about that as Blanche kept talking, "I've been returning the favor to Maria off and on for over twenty years. I thought I had no one back home either, but I was wrong. I should've turned right around and gone back, but I had my stupid young pride. What a waste, but I made my decision that day, and I've lived with the consequences ever since." Blanche added, "Got a place to stay?"

Becky listened very closely to what the worn older woman said. She sensed that she was good. Looking closely, Becky could still see the Iowan in Blanche. One of Becky's classmates in her private high school was from Iowa. Blanche had the farmer look. It wasn't bad; actually, it was a compliment. Farmers are hardworking honest folks.

Becky felt she could trust the older woman. She knew this part of running away would be touchy. Somewhere, she had to trust another person to survive. It was a fifty-fifty gamble, which way it would go. She needed to find a place to live while she looked for a job. Soon her money would run out and that would be it.

"No," Becky answered, "I'm new in town. I'm looking for a room, that I can rent cheaply, maybe an efficiency apartment, but I don't know this town. I don't want to make a mistake or want to get into ANY trouble."

Something organic stirred inside of Blanche. This last sentence rang in Blanche's ear. Instinctively she leaned close and quietly asked, "Honey you still a virgin?" The short-brown-haired girl slowly, shyly nodded her head, as she looked embarrassed. She was embarrassed because the girls at school teased her mercilessly, calling her old-fashioned, 'Princess Prude'.

Becky felt something inside her, something hard to explain. Maybe it was her grandmother's teachings, but she wanted to be with a special man, to marry him, just one man. She thought she was the only girl in her high school that felt that way. It had further isolated her in her gilded prison.

Suddenly, Beck felt anger when she answered Blanche, "Yes, I'm a virgin, and I intend to stay that way until I get married to my husband. Otherwise, I'd rather DIE."

Blanche was surprised at the girl's outburst, but pleased. She'd felt the same way many years ago, only she didn't think there were any more Snow Whites left in these days of casual love.

Blanche smiled, "Look honey, if you can wait another hour, I'll be through my shift, and I know a place where you can stay." Blanche caught the skeptical look from Becky, but Blanche answered, "Yeah, well, this is a place where you'll be safe. I know the man who runs it. I've known him for years. I'd trust my own daughter with him. He charges seventy a week, and you can bring in a hotplate. A motel room in Miami goes for two hundred dollars a night so this guy is cheap."

Blanche stubbed her cigarette out and reached out her hand, "Now that we're friends, what's your name darlin?" Becky hesitated for a minute as she shook Blanche's hand, "My name is – Rebecca Wolefski, but you can call me Becky. I'm from Scranton, Pa."

Blanche answered, shaking her friend's hand, "OK Becky from Scranton. Why don't you go get your bag out of the locker and meet me here? This way, in an hour if you don't show I'll figure you made other plans. If you show, then I'll take you to your room," then Blanche stood up and walked off to finish her shift.

Chapter 2

Becky left the terminal dinner, walking slowly to the lockers where she left her backpack. She sat on a bench for a minute to think. What should I do?

'Should I trust Blanche?' she wondered. 'She didn't know Blanche at all,' but her grandmother had given her advice when they were together all those years ago. Becky had asked, "Grandma how did you know grandpa was the man for you, your man?"

Grandma answered as she brushed a wrinkled soft hand across her young smooth cheek, "A woman develops a sense, a feeling about things in life, Becky. Maybe it's God speaking to us, or a spirit, but the soft gentle voice is the voice a woman listens to. The quiet voice will guide you, keep you safe and make you happy."

Becky sensed from her spirit that Blanche was good. That she was uneducated was evident, but Blanche had a wealth of worldly knowledge, Becky felt. One of her classmates had called this being street smart. Trusting her fate to her inner instincts, Becky quickly retrieved her backpack, went to the ladies' room into a stall, and took a hundred dollars from her shoe. She felt she'd need cash close at hand to buy the things she needed to start her new life. Then she walked back to the terminal dinner.

Blanche brightened when she saw Becky, "I'm glad you decided to let me help you honey. I respect your trust. How do you like your eggs?"

Becky answered, "Dippy."

"Dippy?" Blanched paused and smilingly chuckled.

Becky shrugged her shoulders innocently. That's how her grandmother called the eggs Becky learned to love all those years ago. Grandpa used to say, "If it ain't broken, don't fix it," so she didn't.

Blanche motioned for Becky to sit in her usual stool as she turned to the short order cook, "Roberto, two dippy-eggs, ham slice, toast and jelly please."

Roberto had heard it all, but not dippy, in years. He went about his job.

Blanche filled a cup with hot black coffee, saucer of cream cups, and shortly brought Becky her breakfast.

"I'll just be a minute," Blanched said as Becky finished her breakfast. Shortly Blanche emerged from the kitchen in a pink long sleeve, button front sweater and her purse.

"Where's the check, Blanche?" Becky wondered.

"The breakfast is on me, honey," she said as she took Becky's hand, pulling her out to the terminal's parking lot. There the ninth wonder of the world sat, a seventy-five pink Dodge sedan, with a lime green front fender on the passenger's side. There were dents and scraped-off paint all over the vintage car plus a slightly mangled rear bumper.

Blanche saw Becky's surprised look, "It's paid for honey. Jump in."

Becky wondered if the strange car would run, but the engine turned over like a tuned thoroughbred as Blanche sped her way into the congested traffic. Becky knew Blanche was a gentle person, but when Blanche got behind the wheel of her pink car, another side of the woman emerged. Simply put, she was a horrible driver! She dipped and dove between lines of traffic as she sped off recklessly though downtown Miami.

Becky rolled down the passenger side window, took off her baseball hat, shook out and let the wind play with her chin-length brown hair. 'Oh this is heaven,' she thought enjoying the warm breeze and bright sunshine. She didn't miss the sub-zero temperatures in Chicago. Those sprints from her apartment building to the waiting limousine in the frigid mornings were killers.

The day in Miami was warming up nicely Blanche thought, "Here honey, take the wheel." Becky had never driven a car in her life, but Blanche didn't wait for an answer as she started taking off her sweater, and then took the wheel back from Becky.

"Where did you learn to drive Blanche?" Becky gasped.

Blanche grinned proudly, "Never took a lesson in my life. The first boy I went to the hayloft with taught me how to drive his tractor back on the farm as I sat on his lap, and he plowed the field," she giggled.

Becky put her seatbelt on quietly and instinctively tightened her grip on the arm rest. She gulped as Blanche balleted their pink cruiser in city traffic. She had the same sensation she got every time she was on a roller coaster making the first anticipating climb to the first horrific drop as Blanche drove. Soon she pulled into the Tropicana Motel just off one of the brownish-green back canals.

Without ceremony, Blanch launched out of the car and walked toward the door with "Office" illuminated in fluorescent pink neon sign. Becky followed closely behind. Inside, it took Becky a second for her eyes to adjust. In the relative darkness of the motel office, a balding Latino man in a white wife-beater t-shirt showing underneath an open short sleeve hoola shirt, sat behind the counter watching of all things, soaps! None of this affected Blanche one bit.

"Hello Philpe," Blanche bubbled. "And how is Consuela?"

"Comosta Blanche? Long time no see!" Philpe answered smiling, pleased that Blanche asked about his wife of fifteen years. "Oh Blanche, she is muy bonita, my dove, she is. A man couldn't ask more from life than my Consuela," he smiled as he quickly glanced at Becky then gave Blanche his full attention.

Consuela was Maria's younger sister. Maria was Blanche's mentor when she first arrived in Miami all those years ago. Blanche had watched Philpe grow up as a boy, turn into a man, and marry the sister of her best friend Maria. Now that Maria had passed, Blanche considered herself Consuela's older sister.

Blanche smiled in return, "Philpe, this is my friend Becky. She needs a room. One where she can bring in a hot plate. Is the price still seventy dollars a week?"

Philpe stood, straightened his shirt and looked at Becky, bowing slightly, "That Blanche says you are her friend, makes you my friend also senorita."

Becky did a short courtesy in response that amazed and pleased both Philpe and Blanche. Such pleasantries are rarely seen these days, but for people from a formal Latin culture, manners are a pleasant gift.

Philpe looked back at Blanche, "For a friend of yours Blanche, yes the price, she is still seventy a week, but my boss, he wants cash money and up front. Is this possible?" he looked at both women.

Becky nodded, but Blanche interceded, "Can she see the room first?"

Philpe quickly turned off the TV and took a key from the rack, "I forget my manners, Blanche, my apology. Right this way."

Three doors from the office was room 14. Philpe inserted the key, opened the door and waved the ladies inside adding, "Consuela put clean sheets on the bed just this morning, Blanche. She changes the sheets twice a week, more than that, is a five dollar extra charge."

The room contained a single bed in a main room the size of a large closet, a small table, a bathroom with sink and commode. Philpe turned on an air conditioner in a high window that worked, but there were no other windows.

Apologetically Philpe answered, "Times are hard in Miami these days. Mucho crime, mucho drugs. Many people come here from all over, from Cuba, Columbia, and South America seeking a better life. Most of the people who come here are honest hard-working people, but as in all cultures, in all neighborhoods, there are a few bad people. People with papers," Philpe looked at Blanche, who understood, "can get work, and then others with no papers get what's left," he shrugged his shoulders. "Life is hard either here or back home." Philpe motioned with his head; "We don't have windows so no one can break in. People do what they must to feed themselves or their children."

Blanche looked at Becky, who nodded her approval. Blanche led the way back to the office. Philpe stepped behind the counter to resume his official role.

"Senorita Becky," Philpe began his speech, "the rent is seventy dollars Americano, to be paid in cash every seven days from today. No cash, no room, understand?" Becky pulled out four twenty-dollar bills, handing them to Philpe.

"There is no hooking in my motel, is that understood?" he warned.

Becky blinked, which Philpe took as her understanding. He could see Becky was a good girl, but fortunes in the world could take a terrible turn and a woman might be forced to sell the only thing left she had to sell. This had been the way of the world through time.

"I need your driver's license, senorita," Philpe added.

Blanche answered for Becky, "She doesn't have one Philpe."

Philpe hesitated, "I need some identification Blanche. You know the rules."

Becky nervously braced herself, but Blanche intervened, "Philpe, she doesn't have papers yet," as she raised her eyebrow. "I'm going to take care of that soon."

This time it was Philpe, who nervously announced, "Then it will be ten more dollars a week Blanche, for the silence. You understand."

Blanche knew money smoothed many ills in the world.

She looked at Becky, who nodded. Philpe handed Becky her key, but no change.

Blanche walked back to the room with her new friend. After Becky retrieved her backpack from the car and opened the room's door. Blanche advised, "Get some sleep honey," and handed her a piece of paper. "Here's my number in case you wake up early." Becky didn't need coaxing. As soon as Blanche left, Becky locked the door, pulled off her jeans, pulled back the covers, and she was out like a light. With no windows, it could be day or night.

Becky was awakened from a deep sleep by a knocking at the door, nervously she asked, "Who is it?"

"Its me sleepy head, Blanche. Open up!"

Becky threw back the covers and staggered to the door, cracked it cautiously, seeing her new friend, opened the door to stagger back to the side of the bed, sitting down, trying to wake up.

Becky managed, "What time is it?"

"It's ten am darlin. You slept the clock around," Blanche chuckled.

Blanche took a cardboard cup with a top on it from a bag she held and handed it to Becky. "What's this," Becky asked groggily.

"Be careful not to spill it, it's hot coffee, darlin. Cuban," Blanche answered as she took another cup from the bag for herself as she sat on the bed. There wasn't another place to sit down in the small room.

The rich aroma filled the air as Becky cautiously took a sip. Her eyes began to open as she swallowed.

"Wow!" Becky gasped as she took another long swallow. The wonderful liquid was doing its magic, breathing life back into her tired body.

Blanche laughed, "Is this the first time you've had Cuban coffee?"

Becky nodded as she sipped it slowly and savored the explosion of taste.

Blanche took a long draw on her drink also as she explained, "Cuban coffee is strong, but lightly sweetened. Much like their life."

Becky was coming awake. She listened.

"Miami, is many things," Blanche mentored. "It is beautiful but dirty, rich but poor, all things rolled into one. Miami is like a beautiful tropical rain forest and just as deadly."

They finished their coffees and Blanche threw Becky's jeans over at her, "Get dressed honey, and I'll buy you breakfast."

Becky stepped into her jeans, and she made a hop as she pulled them up that made her chest bounce. Blanche asked, "thirty-eights?"

Becky laughed, "No thirty-sixes. I'm a D, so I look bigger than really I am." Then sobering she confessed, "A large chest can be a blessing or a curse. More often I find it's a curse. I can't sleep on my tummy comfortably AND a man always see 'them' before he ever looks into my eyes."

Blanche drew a hand across her chest dejectedly; "I was at the back of the line when nature passed out chests. I'm a thirty-four minus A."

Becky laughingly gasped, "No!"

Blanche grinned, "I get loads of help from foam rubber. All things in Miami aren't what they seem, suga."

Becky now dressed tied her sneakers, "What's for breakfast? More dippy eggs?"

Blanche crunched the bag the coffee came in and expertly tossed it into the far trash can, "Honey, this is Miami. You are coming from the Midwest, all of this is probably strange. There is a romantic rhythm to the city, to the people," Blanche laughed as she fished out her car keys from her handbag, heading out the door.

Becky got into the passenger's side door and immediately

strapped herself in. Ready for another exciting ride with the Queen of Demolition Derby.

Blanche backed the car out and turned onto the thin, one-way side street leading to a major north, south boulevard lined with brightly painted storefronts of private businesses. The neon colors announced the Caribbean origin of their owners. Suddenly, Blanche swerved over to the curb and stopped her bomb of a car just past the bus stop no parking zone.

On the corner, there was a yellow pushcart trimmed in fire engine red with a yellow umbrella over it to shield the vender from the bright Miami sun. It was approaching noon. All of this was alien to Becky, who just followed Blanche as she approached the vender.

"Good morning, Eduardo, comosta?"

The vender gave Blanche a broad smile, "Life, is good to me, Blanche. The sun is shinning and I'm alive. It is my pleasure to see you this fine day."

Becky wasn't sure what was for breakfast, but these certainly weren't bacon and eggs. The mixture of strong aromas, sweet and pungent made her stomach growl from hunger.

Blanche looked over at Becky, "Honey, Eduardo makes the best Cuban sandwiches in all of Miami. Do you like hot?" Becky blinked as Blanche ordered, "We'll have two sandwiches," Eduardo. "I want a hot one and my friend will have her's with sweet peppers, please."

Eduardo had his ever-present chopping knife and took out a jalapeno, starting to slice it up as suddenly a car screeched to a halt along side them. Two hoodlums ran up to Eduardo, one of the men shoved an automatic pistol in his face, "Give me your money idiota, or you die!"

Blanche through out an arm, pulling Becky behind her. Becky looked around Blanche, wide-eyed, disbelieving what was unfolding before her.

Without pause, Eduardo threw a pan of hot oil on the villain holding the gun then reached out and stabbed him twice in the chest with the chopping knife, almost like a signature. Disbelieving what happened to him, the gunman dropped his pistol, clutched his chest and staggered back against his car in shock."

The gunman's accomplice surprised, but warily eyeing Eduardo and his ever-present knife, helped his gunman friend into the passenger side of the car. Then they sped off as abruptly as they entered the picture. It was surreal.

Even Blanche was speechless, but Eduardo, without blinking an eye picked up the pistol, opened a drawer in his cart already filled with guns, wiped the blood off the butcher knife on his white apron and kept chopping the jalapenos, which he mixed into the pulled pork mixture on his portable hot grill. Expertly, he then used the same knife as a spatula as he cooked Blanche's sandwich.

Blanche stammered, "Eduardo, does this happen to you often?"

Eduardo shrugged, "It happens on the street. One gets used to it, but I need to feed my family. That idiot tried to feed his. I told him NO. Estupido people think I'm an easy mark to rob. He found out different. Where I come from, this happens a lot. To stay in business or even alive, one must deal with it. Most people are like you, Blanche. Honest people experiencing life, but others, like him, try to live life the easy way and follow a life of crime."

Becky silently put a hand to her heart, as she resumed breathing again. Eduardo calmly asked, "Would you like a soda? You are too young for cerveza."

"What flavors do you have?"

Eduardo, the true merchant recounted from memory, "Orange, grape, root beer, papaya, and mango."

Beck, just curious asked, "No cola?"

Eduardo looked like he was a insulted, "Senorita, I am no corporate pimp! I only sell local merchandise that I can vouch for. If you want mierda, you go to them." he angrily pointed his multipurpose chopping knife at the franchised hamburger joint across the street. "Now I'm, an independent businessman," he said proudly.

Becky raised her eyebrows at Blanche, who for the first time, just blinked back at her young friend in silence. Neither woman wanted to rile Eduardo. He still held his very handy chopping knife.

"Orange please," Becky answered gently.

Eduardo smiled, nodded, reaching deep into his cart for an ice-cold orange soda and a beer in a long neck bottle, to which he added a quarter slice of lime across the mouth, handing the beer to Blanche and the orange soda to Becky. From years of experience, he shoveled the pulled pork and peppers into a small smooth roll, sloshed on some secret sauce, then wrapped the sandwiches in waxed paper with the flamboyant flair of a showman.

Blanche paid Eduardo and then the two women took their sandwiches to a bench along the sun-drenched boulevard. Blanche sat on the park bench along the street with her legs spread, in case the sauce dripped. Becky felt like this was truly a vacation, 'all the excitement of Mardri Gras,' she thought.

Blanche took a bite of her sandwich then chased it down with a good pull on her long necked beer as she talked.

"I wanted to ask, Becky, what kind of job are you looking for?"

Becky swallowed, "I'd love an office job, one where I can advance in time."

"Do you have a college degree? Any degree? Any skill?" Blanche asked.

Becky shook her head, "No, but I understand finance some."

Blanche shook her head, "I guessed as much. Honey, you must keep in mind you have a ton of competition out there. All the sorority sisters come down here with their degrees, to party," Blanche winked, "to get a job to pay expenses while they wait for their sugar daddy husband to waltz into their lives."

Blanche had Becky's attention now. Becky became fearful, 'What had she gotten herself into, running away without a skill or degree to pay for her needs?' she thought.

Blanche summed it up for her, "You've got no degree, no real skill, no identification to get a legal job, you want to stay anonymous since you're a runaway and family is looking for you. You've got a voluptuous body, but you're a virgin, and would rather die before you lose it except on your wedding night?"

Becky smiled and shrugged innocently, "Yep, that's about it."

"Wow, " Blanche gasped as she finished her sandwich and drained her beer. She reached into her purse for a short pack of unfiltered cigarettes. She pulled one out, tamped it down, lit it, and inhaled deeply as she thought. Once in the process, Blanche eyed Becky's body and particularly her abundant chest, but seemed to dismiss the thought.

Becky noticed Blanche's lingering stare, "What?" she asked.

"Its TOO RISKY," Blanche replied.

"What?" Becky persisted.

"You have a pair of trump cards Becky, that could be as good as a college degree, but, it's extremely dangerous," Blanche answered sternly.

Becky gave the come-on sign with her hand. Blanche explained.

"There's a place, a night-club here in Miami called the El-Toro. It's a private club, but really it's a social place for a South American drug cartel. The money flows like water there, but the life expectancy is short."

"I've taken some girls there over the years," Blanche took another drag on her cigarette, "but mysteriously they disappear after about four to six months. No trace! Never to be heard from again! I've learned sometimes it's not healthy to ask too many questions," she continued solemnly.

Becky blinked, "You say the girls can last maybe four months, safely?"

Blanche nodded. She dropped the cigarette to the pavement and crushed it out with her black flat shoe.

"Do the waitresses make good money?" Becky questioned.

"They make about 1700 dollars, in cash, a night," Blanche guessed. "Of course there are expenses, but you could clear 1500.

Becky did the math in her head. 1500 a night, times five, that's 7500 a week, times four, 30,000 a month! Times four, is 120,000 dollars in four months. That's a lot of money Blanche!"

"Are you willing to bet your life, Becky?" Blanche asked stoically.

Becky knew Blanche wasn't joking, but then again, the potential gain was overwhelming! She was very unhappy with her life. "Blanche, I'm willing to gamble a short life for a big bank account."

Blanche blinked, "O-K." She thought for a minute. "We need to get you some identification so you can work, and we need to get you some clothes for the interview. Driver's licenses go for a hundred dollars and Social Security Cards go for about four hundred. Can you come up with that kind of cash?"

Without hesitating, Becky nodded, "affirmative."

Blanche gently slapped Becky's arm, "Come-on. We need to get going," she headed back to her car. Becky followed and soon the two were on the move to the barrio of Miami. Becky asked Blanche a question.

"Blanche, if you had money, what would you want?

Without a moments pause Blanche answered, "I've always loved flowers, darlin. My dream is to own a small florist shop, probably in the bus terminal, or maybe an open air shop." Wistfully Blanche looked out the window, "It's a wonderful dream, but I'm resigned it won't ever happen, but the idea gives me hope and brightens my day."

Becky nodded, but didn't say anything. Everyone has their dream, their hope. For some, hope is all they have. It would be a sin to take that from them.

Blanche parked the car in front of row homes in the poor section of town. The facades of the buildings were brick, but worn from years of sun and rain. Wilted flowers drooped in neglected window boxes that evidenced an attempt to bring color in this dull part of town, but had failed. The scene was depressing. Few hopes were visible, but despair was glaring.

Blanche went into one of the doors halfway down the block, and then walked to the fourth floor via the stairs, since there wasn't any elevator. Becky was close on her heels. Blanche squinted at the numbers on the door as if trying to remember something.

She stopped in front of a door and knocked a signal tap. The hairs on the back of Becky's neck stood up as she heard scurrying inside the room as if a rat scampered about, frightened by the knock on the door.

"Ow es it?" a soft male voice asked behind the paint-peeled door.

"We have business to discuss," Blanche almost whispered.

Locks were turned and the door parted a little. A weasel looking man in a clerk's visor put one eye to the opening.

Blanche whispered, "Its me, Fernando. Blanche."

The strange man suddenly remembered her and lightened as if someone had flipped on a switch. The ancient door opened to let the two women in.

Becky was surprised upon seeing inside the room. It was cluttered like a dusty old business office but there was a state-of-the-art computer sitting squarely in the center of a massive oak desk that dominated the room.

"Fernando," Blanche explained, "We need an ID for my friend."

Fernando asked unimpressed, "Do you have the money? Cash money?"

"Is it still a hundred American dollars for drivers license and four hundred for Social?" Blanche questioned.

Fernando nodded, "The price is as always."

Blanche added, "She needs to be twenty-one at least."

Fernando didn't flinch, "No problemo. Whateva you want, I can do."

Blanche looked at Becky, who took off her right sneaker and pealed off five hundred in twenty-dollar bills. That Becky's feet were sweating from the tension and the unaccustomed heat didn't bother Fernando one bit.

Once he was paid, Fernando did his magic. He flipped switches on his computer as the electrical masterpiece was awakened. He was like an orchestra conductor as he performed his tasks.

In two shakes of a lamb's tail, Fernando took Becky's picture, laminated it on an official Florida driver's license and presented her with a brand new United States Social Security card, stating Rebecca Wolefski, now from the street address of the Tropicana Motel, was just twenty-one years old.

The two women nodded to this strange man, goodbye. Then they left.

Walking back to the car Becky asked incredulously, "Are these cards real? Will I get arrested if I show these to anyone?"

Blanche explained, "Fernando was a computer wiz in Bogotá. His family got into trouble with a local cartel, and they were, eliminated. Fernando had old friends who helped him immigrate to the US, and they set him up in business. Fernando pays his benefactors a percent of his business here and all are happy."

Crossing the street, watching for cars, Blanche added,

"Fernando tapped the phone line to the State's computer mainframe in Tallahassee and the Social Security office here in Miami. Yes dear, those cards are as official as they get."

Adding, "The DEA watch the El-Toro night club and catalog all who go in there. They will run an ID check on you the minute, we go into the club's parking lot. I can't afford to bring those people any trouble. They won't take it kindly if people visiting them invite trouble from the Feds."

"Where to next, Blanche?" Becky wondered.

"We need to do some shopping honey." Blanche answered.

Becky didn't mind shopping with Blanche. She was a hoot!

Chapter 3

Blanche and Becky had a whirlwind shopping spree throughout the afternoon. It became very clear to Becky that Blanche knew Miami, particularly the Cuban Quarter, like the back of her hand. More evident was the fact that Blanche had many Latin friends.

Blanched parked her beat-up car along a narrow neighborhood street in front of a small boutique with "Enchantment" written on the front window. Once inside the little shop, two middle-aged women immediately greeted them. Blanche made the introduction, "Lucinda, Miranda, I'd like you to meet my friend Becky, who has an interview at the El Toro tonight."

Lucinda and Miranda bowed slightly toward Becky, who curtseyed out of respect, which pleased the two women. This was a return to the old ways, a gentility of the past. At the mention of El Toro, the two women seemed to tense slightly, exchanging a silent glance, but Becky sensed there was a change in their demeanor, a mentoring attitude, she thought.

Gesturing toward Becky, Blanche outlined, "She needs an interview outfit and also the club's waitress uniform for tonight."

Lucinda and Miranda looked Becky up and down, judging her sizes. Then they started a hushed staccato conversation in Spanish, a slight difference in opinions occurred, but then a consensus leveled as they turned, disappearing deeper into their shop.

Becky had basic clothes in her backpack, but these surely weren't suitable for an interview at the exclusive El-Toro nightclub. Blanche had called and arranged to be at the club by 8 pm that night.

Lucinda had Becky try on a simple A-line knee-length white cotton dress having puffed sleeves with a zippered front and a matching white sweater. A full nylon slip was suggested to wear underneath. The women were expert seamstresses so a slight alteration only took a moment. A half-heeled ankle strap brown leather sandal making Becky a little taller completed the smart looking interview outfit.

The shop also carried the nightclub's cocktail waitress uniform. This outfit consisted of a black polyester body suit, very much like a one-piece strapless bathing suit; complete with inserts, white starched cotton collar & cuffs, finished off with 50s style white cotton wrist-length gloves. Black, three-inch high-heel pumps with half-pointed toe completed the uniform.

This was an opportunity to get some new clothes, since she was going along with her friend to an interview. No one could pass up a chance like this. For her outfit, Blanche chooses a bright yellow tropical, calf-length 50s style skirt and white cotton collared shirt covered also with a white sweater. She slipped on a brown flat healed sandal, as she didn't need more height with her five foot four frame.

Becky and Blanche paid their bills and thanked the ladies for all their help. Leaving their interview outfits on they left the shop turning to walk to a restaurant a few doors down. Blanche checked her watch and saw that it was now 6 pm.

Rico's was a small family restaurante, and they were ushered to a quiet table after a soft-spoken word from Blanche to the hostess. Blanche wanted to go over some important points with Becky. Once seated Blanche ordered.

"My friend will have Papas Rellenas. I'll have the Chicharrones de la Casa. Café con leche now please."

Becky blinked, "Oh, that sounds marvelous. I took four years of Spanish in high school and traveled to Spain two summers ago. I love the culture and traditions," she told Blanche.

"You'll love the food," Blanched promised as their Café con leche and picante were served. They could munch as Blanche covered some issues.

"Becky, the club is very formal and definitely has a hierarchal air to it. You must keep in mind never to look a patron in the eye. That could be taken that you consider yourself equal to them, almost like a challenge that must be answered. Usually a challenge will not end favorably for you. You mustn't talk to any of the patrons, forget what you might hear or see at the club, and I'll recommend you not talking to any of the other employees. All these things could be disastrous. Your life could depend on you obeying these rules. You want to be a beautiful, unthinking fixture. Take your tip money and go home in silence."

Blanche was interrupted as their entrée was served. The symphony of aromas wafted from their warm plates.

Becky put her fork tentatively into her roasted garlic croquettes filled with beef picadillo. The sweet, spicy pepper sauce danced in her mouth as she tried a crispy onion and manchego crème, the sheep milk cheese was heavenly. Although she had an experienced palate, having eaten in the finest restaurants of Chicago, she hadn't had Cuban cuisine before.

Blanche nearly tingled with excitement as she cut off a piece of crisp marinated chicken and added some baked slivers of jalapeno and habanera peppers that ringed the plate as garnish. Her eyes began to tear as she reached quickly for a tissue in her purse to dab her nose as it began to run. She scooped a dollop of sour cream and put that in her mouth. This somewhat quenched the fire blazing in her mouth, "Dang," she half choked, "that's almost better than sex." Barbequed skirt steak and pork masitas, choizo – a Spanish pork sausage flavored with garlic and paprika, and spicy mojo picante – a Cuban sauce made from garlic, citrus juices with olive oil had been drizzled over it all remained on her plate.

Becky looked at Blanche, "Oh this food is wonderful. How did you find this restaurante?"

"Becky," Blanche took a sip of coffee, "Maria took me as a dear friend, that means I was introduced to her family and their friends. The Cuban and Spanish cultures run deep in Miami. They are proud of their heritage and honorable people. I might use the example of Italian's. Cuban, like Italian people have spread out through American cities and discovered their work niche, jobs that can support their families and help their neighbors. As in all cultures, there is a thread of gangster's who deal on the fine line between legal and illegal activities. The people at the El Toro are of the gangster class of people. The upper echelon, the executive class, but they definitely have had a violent history."

Becky listened closely. She had learned of the gangster class of people in society, in different cultures even in Chicago. There are good and bad people in all cultures. She knew a culture couldn't be judged by only a few violent people.

Blanche went on. She stirred her rich coffee with foamy milk and sugar.

"Never speak at the club, unless asked a direct question. Never get friendly with a male patron as this could be considered encroachment on his senoritas or senoras territory. Keep in mind a "hit" in Miami can be paid for by either a man or woman, makes no difference, money is money."

"Is Miami truly as dangerous as you make it out to be, Blanche?" Becky asked aloud. "What about the police? Is the drug traffic that common?"

Blanche sipped her coffee, "The police do what they can. Many people are on the drug lord's payroll. It's easy money, it seems. Some officials are paid handsomely to look the other way. Drugs are only the half of it, Becky. What people desire, they'll pay money to get like: drugs, prostitution, punishment, and worse. Miami, though not much these days, was almost like the cities up north during prohibition. It is nearly impossible to enforce morality by laws. It's a huge waste of money, in my opinion, but that's just me," Blanche confessed.

"I studied Prohibition in school. The government passed a law outlawing alcohol in the 1920s right?" Becky recalled.

Blanche nodded, "And it didn't work. Organized crime supplied and sold alcohol to people who wanted to drink, almost like taking drugs nowadays.   Keeping people from doing what they want, can be near impossible. Prohibition laws were repealed; alcohol was legalized, but controlled. This cut down on: crime, wasted money for police efforts, not to mention prison space, and making alcohol turned into an industry that employed people legally."

Becky saw the parallel. History had repeated itself.

Blanche thought as she ate. An idea blossomed that just might protect her young princess. She grinned, "But would he buy it?" she wondered.

Becky caught Blanches smile, "What?"

"Trust me, Becky. I am trying to make sure you aren't molested while working at the club. That could be difficult, as many of the male patrons at the club have mistresses. These fallen doves have to come from somewhere."

'From the club?' Becky could easily understand.

Blanche cautioned, "Remember, no more than four months, and give a two week notice, then OUT! I don't want you winding up like those other girls I've taken there to work. I hope you're willing to bet your life for that money?"

"Blanche, my life up to this point has been horribly unhappy. I have to make money somehow," Becky countered, after thinking carefully. "I know this a serious decision, but I ran away from an unhappy life evidently unprepared, without documented skills. This was a big chance for me to get a bankroll to finance my new life. Working in a small everyday job would give me enough money to stay at the Tropicana for the rest of my life. I wanted more. I'm willing to gamble to get what I want in life."

"Honey, I'm not sure you know what horribly unhappy is," Blanche looked seriously at her young protégé. "Life can be a living hell, where death could be a blessing. There are things far worse than dying. One can be dead but still living. That would be truly horrible," she thought aloud.

Before more could be said, the waitress came by, cleared the table as Blanche ordered desert. This gave Becky time to think.

Blanche looked at the waitress and recited by heart, as if she were having a religious experience, "dos Tres Lechcs de Banana por fa vor." The waitress nodded and then disappeared like a puff of smoke.

Becky had a questioning look, but waited for her surprise. When the waitress brought two plates, she tasted her treat, but more boldly than with the entrée. She tasted vanilla sponge cake soaked in three banana flavored milks, chocolate banana mousse and caramelized bananas on top." Becky hoped she'd be able to fit into that form fitting uniform when she was done. A saving fact was that the uniform was polyester – stretchy material, she grinned impishly.

The conversation had been sobering, but the dinner was indescribable. She saw the good and the bad of life in Miami. The question was, could she get her money and get out before the tiger ate her?

Blanche noticed the time, motioned for the waitress who brought their check. Becky asked, "How much, Blanche?"

Blanche glanced at the check, took out several bills and put them on top of the check as she gathered her belongings, "When you get some money hon, you can buy me dinner. Tonight, its on me," she answered, getting up from the table. "We need to get moving, it's almost 7:30. Our appointment is at 8 tonight."

Becky followed Blanche's lead as she raised her eyebrows. The dinner was magnificent. She would remember this night for a long time.

The two left the restaurante, walked to the car and both women got in. As Blanche started the car she wondered aloud, "I forgot to ask you, Becky, if you can walk in high heels?"

Becky rolled down her window to enjoy the warm evening's air, "I took four years of ballet. My mother raised me to fit into high society."

Blanche nodded her understanding, "Ballet is good for a waitress. It gives you balance to carry trays of drinks."

Becky looked out at the ethnic shops as they sped by, "Is the El Toro far?"

"The club is in the tourist district. Not far from South Beach," Blanche offered. "When we get to the club hon, remember to only speak when spoken to. Follow my lead and listen carefully. These people are outwardly cultured, but the violence underneath is unimaginable. The place is guarded by a group of bodyguards rivaling a well-disciplined military unit."

Again, Becky said nothing, but her eyebrows arched. Blanche snapped her finger as she turned the corner onto a narrow side street, "We're about to enter the lion's den. Its show time darlin."

The beauty of the El Toro amazed Becky. The club was separated and protected from the street by a reddish brick wall, at least six feet high. On top of the wall was a fence of wrought iron lattice with pointed tops.

"The wall is to protect against any drive-by shooting," Blanche offered.

Becky's heart began to race and her hands grew sweaty. She wondered if she had made the right decision. 'Sure it was a gamble, but the payoff was high,' she thought to herself.

Blanche drove through the gate that got the attention of the three parking attendants and two guards on either side of the entrance. Blanche drove confidently up to the front door and stopped. A man stepped forward smiling, "Senora

Blanche," and opened her door. "It's been a long time. I'm glad to see you again."

Blanche stepped out of the car and patted the man's face, "Ricardo. It's good to see you again also, and how is Rosetta?"

Ricardo's partner opened Becky's door, but stood silently as she exited the beat up dodge. Becky was beginning to become accustomed to Blanche being welcomed by so many people. She also began to realize that Blanche had lived her life in Miami, on the fringe of illegal affairs, no doubt due to Maria's guidance.

Ricardo politely offered, "Oh, Rosetta is fine as are the children. We have another one on the way. God has been good to us, Senora Blanche."

Blanche gently touched his arm, "That's wonderful, Ricardo. Please give Rosetta my best wishes. I'll light a candle for her, praying for a boy this time."

Ricardo's brilliant white teeth smile glowed, but then he sobered, "And what may I ask what is the pleasure of your visit tonight?"

"We have an appointment with Carlos at 8 pm. I am introducing him to a friend of mine," she said as she waved her hand and arm gracefully, indicating Becky.

Ricardo bowed slightly to Becky, but didn't say anything to her. Ricardo nodded to the two guards who looked like hybrids of Chippendale dancers and fashion models stepping from the pages of GQ. Their open jackets didn't hide their rippling muscles and triangular torsos. Becky was stunned, but remained silent as she drew near. The gentle trade wind breeze off the ocean not far away blew the guard's jacket open, and she saw two small sub-machine guns hanging down from a shoulder harness under the expensively tailored jacket.

The other guard spoke into a microphone clipped to his lapel as he held the entrance door open for the two ladies to pass inside. Becky was awed at the thickness of the solid wood door that had a metal plate core at least an inch thick. She thought that the club could double as a fortress if need be.

Once inside, a beautiful woman in a black business jacket and dress walked toward the two women, "Senora Blanche, welcome."

"Yolanda, you have grown to a beautiful woman. Your mother would be so proud of you. You're like a gorgeous flower in spring."

Yolanda beamed, "I will seat you and your friend at Carlos's table. He will be with you shortly. Can I get you ladies some refreshments?"

"Some passion fruit punch please, Yolanda," Blanche answered.

Yolanda waited for the women to be seated at a table for 6 that was illumined by an overhead light that spotlighted a two-foot ring around the table, before she left. Quickly, she returned with two tall glasses of a pink drink with tiny oriental parasols spearing bite-sized pieces of pineapple. Blanche took the parasol from the drink and placed it on a plate, after taking a bite of pineapple and sipping the smooth nectar. Becky did, likewise, surprised by the sweetness of the drink, but strangely drawn to its dance between sweet and tart.

A huge man, about six feet, two hundred pounds at least with coal-black long hair, pulled tightly behind his head in a ponytail that hung down to the top of his shoulders, dressed in a impeccably tailored gray double-breasted suit approached Blanche and Becky. Becky couldn't miss the deep, crowfoot scar on his left cheek. The scar appeared like it had been a 'mark'. Regardless, the scar was loudly disfiguring. Two equally large men dressed in dark suits that blended into the dimly lit atmosphere of the club followed closely, then disappeared into the shadows when Carlos stopped at the table. Twenty empty tables surrounded them, as the club was totally empty at the moment.

Blanche remained seated, but offered her hand to the man

in the gray suit, "Carlos. It was so gracious of you to meet us tonight."

"The pleasure is all mine Blanche, as always. And what can I do for you tonight?" he asked.

"I brought a new acquaintance," Blanche waved a hand indicating Becky, who bowed slightly, respectfully to the older gentleman. "She would like to know if you have an opening for a waitress."

Becky was surprised to hear Blanche introduce her to Carlos as an acquaintance, but then something told her that to say Becky was a 'friend' would've implied vouching for her. *Vouching* in this society could link Blanche to Becky should anything go wrong.

Carlos's gaze shifted smoothly from Blanche to Becky. Becky kept her gaze at chest level, careful not to look at Carlos in the eye as instructed.

Carlos sat down and immediately a steaming cup of Café con leche was placed before him, no doubt his custom when conducting business. He took the spoon from the saucer and stirred the creamy brew in the cup as he thought.

Carlos nodded silently to Blanche, "Stand up Becky," Blanche softly told her. "Let Carlos see you dear."

Becky did as she said and stood up straight beside her chair. Her white outfit was a picture of innocence. "Take off your sweater please," Blanche continued gently as she took the sweater when Becky handed it to her.

Becky did as instructed. Blanche saw the almost imperceptible quaver of his thick black eyebrow. Blanche relaxed a touch.

Blanche saw that Carlos's eyes start with Becky's face, and then proceeded downward to be locked, for a long moment on her abundant chest, to then travel across the rest of her body without stopping.

"You met her at the bus terminal, Blanche?" Carlos asked.

This time it was Blanche's eyebrows that quavered, "You are well informed Carlos."

Carlos shrugged as he took a sip of coffee, "A business man in my position needs to be well informed. People tell me things."

Blanche nodded. She shifted her position.

"She is a runaway?" he continued.

"Yes," Blanche admitted.

Carlos looked at Becky, "Will you be followed?"

"Yes Sir," Becky answered, "but they won't know where to look."

Carlos took another sip of his café. He nodded to Blanche, who handed him Becky's identification cards. He asked, "Fernando?" Blanche nodded.

One of the bodyguards stepped from the shadow to take the ID from Carlos, to do the identity check, disappearing into the darkness. As if choreographed, Yolanda appeared by Becky's right side. Blanche directed, "Go with Yolanda, Becky. Change into the uniform please."

Becky bent down demurely, without saying a word and picked up the brown leather bag that contained her uniform items. She followed Yolanda, who took her to a brightly lit room with a large picture mirror, "Change here. I'll be waiting outside when you're ready," Yolanda announced, closing the door.

Becky quickly changed into the waitress uniform. When she was finished, she looked into the picture mirror at her make up, touched up her lipstick and then clicked to the door in her new high heels.

The three inch heels added to her only five foot height, but they popped out Becky's already athletic calves and perked up her behind. She opened the door to the changing room and Yolanda stepped forward, escorting her back to the table. Once back with Blanche and Carlos, Yolanda disappeared into the darkness of the club.

As Blanche previously directed, Becky first faced Carlos, but very careful not to look in his face, then turned one-quarter turn after counting to ten, until she made a complete circle. This gave Carlos a good look at her in her uniform.

"Is this catching?" Carlos's brow wrinkled as he looked at Blanche.

Blanche leaned toward Carlos and whispered. Carlos looked at Becky, but clearly he was looking at her front, weighing his thoughts. Finally, he stretched out his right hand and a black cape was draped over his arm. Carlos handed the cape to Blanche, "Tomorrow night is New Years Eve. She can start then. Have her here by 9 pm and report to Celeste. Celeste can train her."

"Yes Carlos, and thank you for your time," Blanche responded, standing and then walking to Becky's side. Yolanda reappeared from the darkness, but took Becky to another room, one that didn't have a mirror in it.

Blanche helped Becky change and then Yolanda escorted the two women to the entrance of the club where Blanche's beat-up dodge was waiting, with open doors. Without fanfare, Blanche got into the car and drove off.

Becky was full of questions, but Blanche silently held her finger to her lips until she had driven to a park near by, stopped the car and got out to sit on a picnic bench. Becky followed. Once she was seated, Blanche reached into her purse, took out a new pack of Lucky Strips, twirled the red starter cellophane to open the pack, pealed back the foil and tapped out a smoke. Expertly, she lit it and took a deep drag on the unfiltered cigarette. She held in the smoke for a long pause and then exhaled slowly, smoke trailing from her nostrils.

Becky couldn't contain herself, "Well? How did it go?"

Blanche took another deep drag, "Carlos liked you hon, as much as Carlos likes any female."

Becky looked confused, "You don't mean Carlos is?"

Blanche chucked, "No darlin, he's not gay, but Carlos

doesn't get close with anyone except Carlos. Women to Carlos are a means to an end." She shrugged, "in many different ways. Carlos is a complicated man. Someday when we have a lot of time and a full bottle of light rum, I'll explain Carlos to you."

Becky gasped, "Did you see that scar?"

Blanche nodded, "Only a blind man could miss that. That scar was put there on purpose. Carlos was tortured for information when he was young, working his way up through the ranks in his cartel. Carlos refused to tell any secrets and his face was horribly slashed. He would have been carved to pieces, but was rescued by his crew, who saved his life. That scar reminds Carlos of loyalty, and that torture can be an effective tool to get information. Torture, he knows, is inflicting excruciating pain without killing the person being questioned."

Blanche crushed out her cigarette, "I wasn't sure if the car was bugged, since they had the car while we were in the club. What I have to tell you, some of it is vitally secret."

Becky leaned close. She didn't want to miss a single word.

"That you have been hired," Blanche rested her elbows on her knees, "is evident. The cloak Carlos gave me is your 'safe passage' anywhere in the city."

Becky looked confused, "I don't understand."

Blanche held up the black cape. Becky saw a huge raging bull on the back and over the left breast. El Toro was embroidered in gold thread, easily seen at night. This cape means that you are a member of the El Toro family. If you are harmed, the offender has harmed 'the family' and will be dealt with mercilessly."

Becky nodded. She was starting to understand.

"You work until three or four am, the buses don't run that late or early, depending on how you think about it. When you walk the ten blocks home to the Tropicana Motel, you will wear the cape and no one will bother you. See?" Blanche asked. "You are now owned by the El Toro nightclub Becky."

This thought sent a shiver down her spine. "Owned?" she thought.

In a minute she recovered enough, "What did Carlos mean, is it catching?"

Blanche half laughed, "I told him you said you had herpes, but only in a 'certain' place. He asked if it were catching? I whispered, "No, unless someone puts something in, that's not supposed to be there."

Becky sat silently, blinking. Then they both got back into Blanche's car, and she drove Becky to the Tropicana in Little Havana and kissed Becky goodnight.

"I have to work tomorrow, so you'll be on your own. Get to the club by 9 pm," Blanche reminded as she went home herself.

Chapter 4

The next day, New Years Eve, Becky walked up to the El Toro nightclub, with her backpack and cape at 7:30 PM. She was early, but she surely didn't want to be late for her first day on the job. The minute she walked through the gates, five sets of eyes locked onto her as a possible threat, not for her looks. Ricardo approached her as she neared the club's entrance.

"Yes senorita Becky, can I help you?" he asked.

Becky was amazed, he remembered her name, "I'm here to start work Ricardo. Last night I was hired as a cocktail waitress and was told to report for work at 9 pm. That Celeste is going to train me."

Ricardo held up his finger for a moment and stepped back away from her, speaking into an imperceptible microphone attached to an earpiece. He must have been speaking to someone inside, confirming Becky's story. "Si," Ricardo said to the invisible person on the radio. Then turning to Becky, "You may go in senorita. They are expecting you," gesturing to the side entrance.

Becky cringed fearfully after she said cocktail waitress without thinking. She hadn't known many boys, but the ones she did, were of the jock mentality. They would've made crude jokes about her statement. Thankfully there hadn't been any of that from Ricardo. Strangely, he had been all business. She was starting to see that this place was run very professionally, with high classed people, behaving with military-style discipline.

She walked to the side entrance, through the doors and into a small foyer. The foyer had tan walls with dark wooden trim. The floor was 1950s style black and white checkerboard linoleum. A handsomely dressed hunk of a man stood behind a maitre d's tall wooden podium commonly seen in restaurant entrances, "Name?" the guard politely asked.

"Becky Wolefski," she answered.

"Celeste will be by in a minute, Becky. Please have a seat," the man indicated a bank of plush brown leather seats against the wall.

She did as she was told and sat down. She could see the man's side profile and his jacket was unbuttoned. She got goose bumps when she saw his shoulder holster with an automatic pistol in it. It seemed all male employees at the club were armed. 'Wow,' she thought, 'this really different than anything I've known before, except in a bank.'

Becky had a chance to think about the building that enclosed the El Toro. The clubhouse was a Spanish version of a Victorian style hacienda or rural planter's mansion. The building had to have been originally built in the early 1900s, when Miami Beach was young and there'd been plenty of space to build. Now, this real estate would be worth a fortune for the land alone.

Inside the El Toro was a contrast of ultra modern to remaining old. Systematically, the building was being renovated, updated with sparkling new metal work and state of the art lighting. She sensed that this club, like its members, was in a metamorphosis. This drug cartel was evolving into nouveau riche. Maybe the club members now were outwardly flaunting their windfall profits from the explosion in drug trade of the 1960s and 70s. Blanche had told her about 'the old days'.

Evidently, in the 1960s and 70s when the drug trade was almost wide open, millions in cash were made. Bank branches opened overnight to accommodate large deposits, but the home bank might be one located somewhere in the Central America, or in Panama. By the 1980s, law enforcement had cracked down on the illegal drug smuggling and made this form of business very hazardous. Now days, the cartel was moving into other illegal activities or even becoming legitimate. The cash flow from drugs was greatly reduced, but surely not eliminated according to the all-knowing Blanche.

The clicking sound of high heels on linoleum brought Becky back to reality. A shapely long-legged blonde woman who looked fit enough to be a former collegiate cheerleader, now in her mid-twenties, dressed in club waitress uniform stopped at the podium to chat with the dreamy-looking guard. He pointed toward Becky with a gesturing nod of his head.

The blonde clicked over, "Becky?"

Becky stood up, "That's me," she answered.

"Hi, I'm Celeste, head waitress here at the club," she said.

Becky smiled, "Nice to meet you."

The two women looked like a comical pair. Celeste was five feet eight at least and Becky conversely was five feet even.

Celeste relaxed a touch from her initial professional demeanor, "You're in luck. Donna, one of our other waitresses, called out sick tonight, and we're short handed. New Years Eve is the busiest night of the year, except for Marti Gras." Celeste looked at Becky seriously, "Are you ready to make some money?"

Becky shot back without hesitation, "Sure am!"

"Have you ever been a waitress before?" Celeste asked.

Becky shook her head, "No, but I'm a fast learner."

Celeste could see this new girl was energetic and smart. She saw good things for Becky if she minded her own business and her mouth shut.

"Ok, let's get going," Celeste said as she started off at her usual fast walk. Becky picked up her backpack and cape, hurried to keep up with her teacher.

"I'm going to take you to a room to get changed" Celeste started. "Then you'll shadow me as the night gets going. If you catch on, I'll give you a table to watch and see how you do. OK?"

"Do we change in that room with the big picture mirror in it," Becky asked.

"No," Celeste answered flatly but firmly.

When Becky didn't answer, Celeste dropped a secret. "That room has a two way mirror in it."

Becky hesitated, then kept after Celeste, "You mean people watched me change my clothes during the interview?"

Celeste felt a little sorry for Becky, "You were taped changing. Some of the bosses get a thrill seeing a new girl in her lingerie or nude, but there are other reasons too." Celeste didn't explain further and Becky didn't press.

Becky flushed. She'd never been nearly naked in front of men before. 'OH, how humiliating!' she cringed.

Celeste stopped in front of a door with a skirted figure on it for women and pushed the door opened. Becky saw that the room was plain, with bench seating, and lockers against the wall. "This is where the girls' change. When you're dressed, go back to the foyer. In ten minutes, we'll have inspection."

Becky looked puzzled, but didn't say a word. Celeste answered her questioning look.

"All evening shift employees gather for roll call and inspection at 9:30 pm each night. The club officially opens for business at 10. Should someone not show up for work, her or his work assignments are rearranged at that time."

'That was logical,' Becky thought, 'very efficient.'

Celeste walked off crisply down the hall. She had oodles of things to do before the club opened. Becky went into the room, changed into her waitress uniform, stored her things in the locker, then made her way back to the foyer as instructed.

Other employees, female and male were gathering. Strangely, no one talked or gossiped like other groups. Becky felt the tension, but more, there was an undercurrent of 'caution'? She followed everyone's lead and stayed quiet, just nodding silently, but politely as everyone waited.

The bartenders were dressed in crisply starched white

cotton form fitting shirts, black bow ties, with black slacks. Some bartenders wore wife-beater under shirts, some wore t-shirts, and several didn't wear undershirts at all. Becky could see 'they were cold,' she giggled to herself. However, she looked at them, these bartenders were a breath-taking group of males. Not one of them weighed less than one hundred ninety pounds, with rippling abs, and having maybe six percent body fat?

Celeste and what appeared to be her male counterpart or head bartender strode down the hallway together from the dinning area toward the foyer. There the pair split. The head bartender inspected his troops, and Celeste took role and made sure all her girls' uniforms were acceptable by club standards.

Becky felt this whole group performed very much like a well-organized team. There wasn't any fooling around with this bunch she could see.

She quickly learned that most communication in the club was by hand signals. Celeste pointed at Becky with her index finger to follow, as she headed back to the dance floor-table room to begin their night's work. Becky could easily see that once the band started playing, normal conversation would be near impossible. She also sensed that this background noise would hide any secret conversations from others who shouldn't hear. Everything at the club was very carefully planned. Nothing was left to chance.

Members started arriving at the club about 10:30 pm, mostly as couples, but there were a few single males. Everyone seemed to know everyone, if only as acquaintances.

Celeste took over Donna's three-table assignment. Becky followed Celeste, staying on her left side and slightly behind.

Becky saw that the main floor of club bordered the dance floor on three sides. It seemed that this floor was reserved for junior cartel bosses and their female companions. There was a balcony, with only four tables, that were reserved for senior bosses. The single males were older men who intermingled with the couples sitting in the balcony. An elaborate bar ran the entire length of the back wall, under the balcony overhang.

Becky noticed that the mixed drinks ordered by the males that weren't straight alcohol, had hugely macho names like hatchet, machete, shotgun. The female members ordered drinks with characteristic feminine sounding names like tulip, mimosa, or sunrise.

Each time Celeste served a round of drinks, one of the junior bosses would tip her with at least a fifty-dollar bill. One hundred dollar bills weren't uncommon. The club seemed to run on a credit system, where each member's drinks were written down and the tabs were paid for at the end of the night, in cash. The bosses liked to try to impress each other by tipping in ever increasing amounts of money. It was almost like boasting how affluent they had become.

Halfway through the night, Celeste let Becky take a table on her own. The club did offer a small food menu, but entrees listed were snacking finger foods, nothing too heavy for her to carry. Becky was amazed that she could handle the work, to watch her patrons, and help them enjoy their social agenda.

The seven hour work night simply flew by. Before she knew it, she was dressed in street clothes, with her backpack and red El Toro cape on, walked the ten blocks from Miami Beach back to the Tropicana Motel in Little Havana. Her feet were incredibly sore from her high heels, but Celeste was happy with her help and ability. She gave Becky three hundred in cash, a part of Celeste's tip money. Celeste made almost two thousand dollars that night, but she first had to pay her assigned bartender his usual two hundred dollars, for his night's help.

As soon as Becky got back to the Tropicana, she stripped off her jeans and fell into bed. The sun was just starting to rise in the east. It was 5 am on New Years Day.

A tapping on the door woke Becky from a sound sleep. She staggered to the door, cracked it, and then saw Blanche's grinning face. She opened the door to let her friend in the small room the size of a shoe box. Then Becky gingerly padded her way back to the side of the bed to sit. "What time is it?" she yawned, still half asleep and her feet ached.

Blanche held out a steaming cup of Café con leche. The aroma was heavenly. Becky took the cup carefully, not to spill the brew and burn herself. She was starting to love this light, but sweet blending of rich strong coffee, light cream combined with sugar. It was like a desert in a cup.

"It's noon hon." Blanche bubbled. Blanche was a day person, usually up by 3 am and starting her day's work at 5 am at the bus station dinner. Becky was on the opposite schedule starting her workday at 9 pm.

Blanche looked around, "Gosh Becky this room is so small," she said as she sipped her coffee. "Come on sleepyhead, wake up," Blanche coaxed electrified with excitement, "I've got a surprise I want to show you."

Looking through blood-shot eyes, irritated from the smoke of the club, Becky looked up, "What surprise?"

Blanche laughed with a good belly laugh, "Well if I told you pumpkin, then it wouldn't be a surprise, right?" Blanche threw Becky her jeans, "Get dressed."

Becky took a long sip of her coffee, put it down on the one table in the closet sized motel room, to slide into her jeans. She tied on her sneakers, and in a minute, both women were in Blanche's car. Blanche crossed Macarthur Causeway from Little Havana back into Miami Beach. She turned onto 5th street, left on Ocean Drive, and stopped in front of a brand-new huge skyscraper.

The tall building took up a city block, right on the beach. It had a central core, but also featured a covered walkway around the building at street level.

Blanche got out of her wreck of a car and walked to the right of the building with Becky following close on her heels. They went around the building under the overhang, passing the chic boutiques at the street level. This was like a strip mall all the way around the building. One could live in the building and go shopping without needing a car. Blanche walked to the back of the building where they saw a guard sitting at a stairway leading directly onto the beach.

The view of the ocean and beach was awesome. Puffy clouds drifted by against a light blue sky and the deeper blue of the Atlantic Ocean. Becky thought this was the ultimate opposite of the Lake Michigan view back in frosty Chicago.

Blanche grabbed Becky, striding arm in arm back into the skyscraper, into an ultra contemporary lobby and up to a bright yellow-blond-toned front desk. A female clerk greeted them, "How may I help you ladies today?"

Blanche asked excitedly, "Can we see the sample apartment? Is it still on the fifteenth floor?"

The attendant nodded and reached behind her to get the key, "Yes, apartment 1504 is our example apartment."

Blanche hurried off to the elevators, holding Becky's hand, and almost pulling her. This was a party for Blanche. She was having a ball. Becky hadn't seen such architectural beauty up close since leaving Chicago, although this was a different style of building than she was used to. The structure had a light Caribbean or Latin flavor to it where the apartment building in Chicago had a heavy mid-western feel.

In minutes the elevator whisked the two women to the fifteenth floor. Blanche seemed to know what she was looking for. She turned to the right as she got off the elevator and quickly found the apartment.

Blanche excitedly presented Becky the apartment key to open the door. Becky did the honors, unlocked the door, and pushed it open. Both women gasped in awe. The apartment seemed to unfold like a flower before them. As one opened the front door into an atrium like a base, a slight hallway like a stem drew one into the apartment's main area, which was very open with a high ceiling unfolding like the blossom of the flower.

The interior of the apartment was ultra modern with a crisp clean feel. Powder gray plush weave wall-to-wall carpet cushioned one's step. The walls were painted a light almond color, which absorbed some of the abundant sunlight that streamed in through the three floor to ceiling picture windows. The hallway opened up into the main living area that faced the Atlantic Ocean in front, and north and south Miami Beach to the left and right.

Becky was stunned. She hadn't ever seen anything like this before. The architect surely knew what she was doing, featuring the magnificent view as a panoramic painting that continually changed depending on the time of day. The three walls in front and to her sides, were completely open with a wall of clear glass, allowing the occupant to fully taste with their eyes the beautiful azure blue Atlantic Ocean and exciting Miami Beach.

The apartment was furnished in contemporary design; the matching sofa and lounging chairs were covered in soft black velour accented in gleaming chrome. An open kitchen, behind and to the left of the main sitting area would make any master chef feel at home, featured a restaurant grade gas stove, black marble countertops on gunmetal gray wood cabinets. The bedroom was to the right of the entry hallway, furnished with a queen-sized bed, and was walled off to allow total darkness even in the middle of the day. The apartment designer catered to the Miami Beach elite, who worked at night, but allowed the tenant to sleep in complete darkness well into the day.

Becky ambled into the master bath that was attached to the bedroom. It had earth tone ceramic tiled walls of dark brown, black, with cream sparkles. The stand up shower, the old-fashioned four-legged tub, vanity/sink counter top, commode and bidet were color coordinated in a midnight black theme. Inside the bathroom, one had the feeling of being snugly wrapped in a warm cocoon.

Blanche was anxious to show Becky one more amenity of the apartment. She took Becky to the skyscraper's roof.

The elevator's doors opened to a glass-enclosed lobby. A handsomely athletic male attendant served as both a host and guard, being openly armed.

"May I help you ladies?" he asked.

Blanche strangely knew the routine, "We're from apartment 1504 and want to see our rooftop space," indicating a cypress plank wall divided into cubicles that cut off the ocean view".

The guard saw Becky held the 1504 key then waved his hand toward the back wall, "Enjoy yourselves."

Blanche walked toward the wall of doors, stopping in front of 1504 and waited for Becky to open this door too. "Oh MY," escaped from Becky's lips.

Both women looked into the cubicle to see a hot tub, surrounded on three sides with cypress wood walls with an open top to allow an unobstructed view of the sky. The ocean front wall was of glass, allowing the patron to privately enjoy their hot tub combined with being able to gaze far out into the Atlantic Ocean.

Blanche didn't waste a second, "Since we're here," she giggled, "we might as well enjoy ourselves." Becky and she were good friends now. She didn't see a reason to be modest, so she closed and locked the door, then started to undress. Becky thought, 'Why not!' and soon joined Blanche already relaxing in the warm bubbling pool.

After a minute Becky smiled, "I'm afraid to ask the price of this place."

"Depends what cost you're asking about," Blanche returned, with her head back against the padded headrest looking up at the soft blue sky.

"To rent of course," Becky shot back, "Gosh, the apartment

complete, at this address, with this view, has to cost about a million to buy."

Blanche grinned, "Not quite. Try five million."

Becky jerked with surprise, "NO WAY."

Blanche explained, "Since the drug boom of the seventy's, peons have a million dollars these days. The cartel that owns this building and the bank inside, to launder their drug money by the way, wanted to keep the address exclusive, hence the five million dollar price tag.

Becky shrugged, "At least we got into their hot tub before going back to the Tropicana," she sighed.

Blanche grinned a cat-swallowed-the-canary smile, "not so fast. There are different ways to look at everything," she pointed out.

Becky turned her head. This had to be good.

"Everyday people can rent the apartment and this roof top spa for fifteen thousand a month. But," Blanche hinted.

"But what?" Becky wondered.

Blanche smiled, "Since you work at the El Toro, waitresses can rent this apartment for a thousand a month."

"No-way!" Becky gasped.

Blanche gave her affirmative head shake silently. In little while the women got out and dried themselves off with thick towels folded on a table. Blanche answered Becky, "All of this comes with an army of attendants Becky, you know. The apartment is cleaned; your sheets are changed daily by several maids who also maintain this spa."

Becky was starting to understand, but Blanche explained, "The El Toro wants you healthy and happy, stress free so you can do your job at the club. The apartment comes fully furnished. Do you want to rent this place, suga?"

"Who wouldn't?" Becky exclaimed.

Becky hugged Blanche in excitement, the thrill of finding a nest of her own. Then they ambled back to the main lobby, returning the key to the same sorority sister desk clerk.

Blanche asked the clerk, "Can waitresses from the El Toro still rent this apartment for a thousand a month?"

At the mention of the El Toro, the attendant stiffened a little. Her Daddy had called in a lot of favors to get her this job from the high-rise owners. The corporation who owned this skyscraper also owned the El Toro nightclub. She had been in Miami long enough to know there are certain people not to fool with. The El Toro crowd was definitely in this category.

"Yes Ma'am," the attendant answered.

Blanche indicated Becky, "My friend is a waitress there, and she'd like to rent the 1504 apartment with the roof top spa."

The attendant was perturbed, jealous to say the least. She'd only heard of the roof top hot tubs with the spectacular view. She asked snootily, but with a charming smile, "Does your friend have proof of employment at the El Toro? A pay stub perhaps?"

Blanche was getting annoyed by the haughty twit, "Well bless your heart... No, no pay stub, but you can call the club and ask for Carlos Hernandez. I'm sure he'd LOVE to answer ANY questions you may have," she flashed a peaches and cream smile.

The desk attendant hadn't been on the job long, but long enough to know there are things to do and not do. One of the other girls working on the desk had called an unlisted number once. The next day she didn't show up for work.

The clerk retreated, "Please have your friend fill out the registration form. The day manager can verify her employment, but I'll need one thousand dollars now please to secure the lease.

Blanche was on familiar ground. Without hesitation, "My friend hasn't been paid yet. Give her the key and she'll drop off the money later this week."

The clerk fidgeted uncomfortable. She wasn't sure what to do.

Blanche repeated, "Give her The Key. IF your bosses have a problem with Becky, they or their associates, certainly know where to find her."

The clerk handed Becky the key with a gulp. She understood. She had heard that the building's owners had an effective collection agency on retainer.

Blanche wasn't finished with this biach yet, "My friend also wants to open a checking and savings account with the Banco de Antiwa. The savings account is the private offshore one paying thirteen percent interest rate. She will be making frequent cash deposits," Blanche smiled and batted her long eyelashes.

The clerk silently, but mechanically, got the application forms as she smiled, pushing the forms toward Becky. Blanche thought, 'if the clerk's eyes were daggers, we'd be dead.'

The clerk told Blanche haughtily, "Your friend needs to deposit some money to open the account."

Annoyed, Blanche told Becky, "Give her, a fifty."

Becky reached into her ragged jean's pocket and took out a crisp fifty-dollar bill. She put the money on top of her application. The clerk batted her eyelashes nervously as the two contrasting women left the lobby. "Must be an old Madame and one of her young whores,' the clerk thought as the two women left.

"Blanche," Becky questioned in a hushed tone as they left the building, "Why does El Toro allow waitresses to rent the apartment with no collateral?

Blanche lit an unfiltered Cammel, exhaling, "Darlin, you are the collateral."

Chapter 5

That night Becky went to work. After she'd changed into her uniform in the ladies locker room, Celeste met her the moment she came out, "Becky, something came up. Can you take over Donna's set of tables tonight? You did very well last night. Your patrons were impressed with your service."

"I'd be glad to help anyway I can, Celeste," Becky told her, but also wondered, "Will this just be for tonight? Will Donna be coming back soon?"

Celeste tensed a bit, "No, these tables will be yours from now on. Donna has, moved on," she blinked.

Becky's new set of tables was toward the dance floor, and to the left. She saw that young couples mainly occupied this area, as if they were just starting out in the 'corporation' like junior executives. Some were married evidenced by wedding and engagement rings; others were "escorts" of the often flamboyant young single bosses trying to make a reputation for themselves.

Strangely, Becky started remembering instructions her mother had given her about business relations. She started using some of her instincts.

Becky was pleased that she had the ability of total recall, this as a forte' of her's. She could clearly remember who ordered which drink at each of her three tables. It was common for a young boss to shout, "A round of drinks!" Some waitresses ran into problems, since they couldn't remember who ordered what. This was an area where she excelled.

Becky was a born hostess. Her mother had taught her to be aware of her surroundings, the people at her party, and their condition. All these lessons and skills started to come in handy.

She soon realized that higher bosses in the nightclub were looking closely at the young bosses and their dates. The young bosses were on guard, about how they and their dates appeared to others. It was almost as if the junior executives were being judged for promotion, to see if they could handle greater responsibilities within the cartel. Becky realized that greater responsibilities meant higher pay.

The call of, "A round of drinks," would be recorded for the boss to pay his tab at the end of the night, but waitress tips were paid in cash. The baseline tip was usually a fifty-dollar bill.

Becky soon started to recognize regular club members, especially members who seemed to sit at her tables. One night she saw a young boss and his senorita making their way toward her table, but the young boss kept stopping to chat with other bosses, going out of his way to be 'social'.

By the time the couple arrived at her table, Becky had their usual drinks waiting for them as they sat down. After the first round of drinks, Becky saw that the senorita was starting to get tipsy. Maybe she hadn't had anything to eat and the alcohol was overly affecting her, but something was wrong. The senorita had been drinking rum and cola. On the second round of drinks, Becky watched the senorita's eyes flicker, as she tasted just cola, no alcohol. Since the drink was dark, no one could tell the difference. Becky also arrived with a salsa and cheese platter, announcing, "compliments of the house."

The young women were as sharp as their Dons. If their men advanced, so did the women's wealth also. The senorita knew the club and that Becky had purchased the food to help her, so she wouldn't make a drunken scene. The senorita silently nodded her thanks to Becky, who quickly dropped her eyes to maintain her servant's posture. The senorita whispered to her man, her Don. After that, Becky's tips changed from fifty to one hundred dollar bills.

Evidently, the women in the club 'talked' to each other.

Word spread that Becky was a quiet, competent young woman, not a threat, but often ready to help. She noticed that her tips stayed at one hundred dollars from then on, even with other couples.

Becky had taken four years of Spanish in high school, even traveling to Spain in her junior year for a summer. At first she didn't understood what people were saying in Miami, even though it sounded like Spanish. As she spent more time here, she realized people were speaking a patois or dialect of Spanish, and then she started to understand more conversations.

As she served drinks at her table, a young ambitious Don, Don Antonio, was constantly talking about another higher-level Don, Don Miguel, almost idolizing the older man. The problem was that a higher Don couldn't stoop to socialize with a Don of lower status. Becky had seen this at her mother's country club all too often, but she knew the solution.

Becky went to the waitress of Don Miguel, slipped her a fifty under the table, telling her that her Don, Don Antonio would be honored to buy Don Miguel a drink. Becky had paid the fee for crossing waitress turf. Next, Becky slipped the other waitress's bartender another fifty to order Don Miguel's usual drink. The bartender took out a special bottle of rum, rum from Don Miguel's province.

Becky then delivered the drink to Don Miguel, explaining that Don Antonio hoped that Don Miguel was enjoying the evening as much as Don Antonio was. Don Miguel took a sip of the drink, noting his special formula and nodded to Becky. Then Don Miguel walked over to talk to Don Antonio, with his drink still gripped in his hand, which stunned Don Antonio.

Evidently, Don Antonio had wanted to pitch a business deal to Don Miguel that would be mutually profitable, but protocol was delaying a meeting. The delay could mean losing the business opportunity. Once Don Miguel heard Don Antonio's idea, plus the fact that they both were from the same neighborhood back in Columbia, soon both Dons were talking like long lost cousins.

Don Antonio learned of Becky's role in his meeting Don Miguel. This was a gutsy move on her part and could've been disastrous. Lady Luck smiled on both that night and all had gone well.

As the tables emptied at the end of the night, Don Antonio sent his date on ahead with friends as he hung back to talk to Becky. He motioned Becky over as he took a fist-full of crisp bills from his pocket. This time, Don Antonio opened his wad fully and took three bills from the center, putting the bills on Becky's serving tray deliberately as his final tip of the evening, "Thank you, Becky for your help. You took a huge chance for me, but I reward good service and loyalty."

Becky said nothing and never looked up. She remained neutral, curtseying slightly. Don Antonio paused, then moved on. She was stunned cold when she saw that the bills on her tray weren't hundreds, but rather were thousand dollar bills! None of this went unnoticed. Things aren't always, as they appear to be.

Events started to speed up as the days passed. Girls in turfs higher than Becky were leaving unexpectedly. She was soon promoted to tables that catered to higher-level Dons, as new girls took over the tables, she once had.

As Becky became comfortable with her surroundings, she started seeing the club through new eyes, as if a veil of fog was clearing. Constantly, events at the club moved ever forward.

She saw that Celeste seemed to spend her spare time close to a dark stranger. A man she didn't know. This stranger never brought a senorita to the club, but he always sat on a stool at the quiet end of the bar. In time, she heard one of the waitress gossip that Celeste was Raul's pet.

Becky kept her eye on Raul, Raul Mendoza. The next night, the tables of the gossiping waitress were strangely unattended. Again, Celeste promoted Becky.

One night, Celeste and Raul were having a quiet conversation enjoying their time together, when suddenly a waitress shrieked from the main floor. Celeste raced away from Raul's side to see what was the matter. A single Don, somewhat drunk, had put his hand where it shouldn't have been on his waitress who shrieked, causing a scene.

From the corner of her eye, careful not to look openly, Becky saw Raul's nod to Carlos. Bouncers soon escorted the drunk Don quietly from the club. Becky never saw the drunken Don again. From this, she saw that Raul was truly the brains and power behind the El Toro. Carlos was merely the enforcer.

Celeste escorted the waitress who caused the scene from the main floor. The next night her tables were open and the waitress next in line advanced.

Becky's bank account had grown exponentially. Now it amounted to almost 96,000! That morning she took the page off the daily calendar. April 1st appeared. She never gave it a thought.

Becky often would do Don's innocent favors. That night at the club, a Don asked her to see what was keeping his senorita. She had gone to the ladies' room.

When Becky walked into the ladys', she heard someone being sick in a stall. "Senorita? Your Don wants to leave," Becky spoke at the closed door of the stall. The senorita continued being violently ill. "Are you alright?" Becky asked with increasing concern.

An ashen-faced young woman opened the stall door and wobbly, walked to the sink. She rinsed out her mouth.

"Are you ill senorita? Should I call a doctor?" Becky offered.

"By the saints, don't do that! Jefe would find out!" the young girl answered terrified.

"But you're sick," Becky admonished.

The young girl moaned, "I forgot to take my pills, I'm pregnant."

Neither Becky nor the young senorita heard the older woman enter the ladys'. They were too focused on their problem.

"If Jefe finds out, he'll send me to The Farm!" she exclaimed terrified.

The older woman cleared her voice, "Becky, go back to your tables. I'll take care of her." From the stern tone in the older woman's voice, this wasn't a request, but rather an order.

Becky did as she was told, but she kept an eye on the ladys' room door. When the older woman came out, her Don met her and the younger senorita. The older woman must have explained what happened inside. The older Don signaled a single Don, who escorted the younger woman from the club. Carlos appeared from out of the shadows, who conferred with the older Don.

At closing, Carlos the imposing giant barred Becky's way; "I understand a senorita said something to you in the ladys' room?"

Becky looked at Carlos's chest, "I didn't hear anything, Sir. I was sent in there by a Don to check on his senorita. She was sick, was all. An older senora helped her, and I returned to my duties."

Carlos put a finger under Becky's chin, lifting her face, "Are you sure that was all that happened?"

Becky looked directly into Carlos's eyes and answered flatly, "Yes Sir. That's all that happened."

Carlos took two bills from his pocket and put them on Becky's serving tray, "We appreciate your service and loyalty," he told her.

Becky curtseyed. She never replied.

Strangely, Carlos turned and walked over to two bouncers

who stood on either side of Celeste, then Carlos and a Celeste, uncommonly stiff and tense, left the club escorted.

Becky had time to think about what had happened on her walk home that night. She realized that the only waitress position higher than her own was the one held by Celeste. She sat on a bench by the ocean watching the sun come up. As the sun rose in the sky, so did a feeling of dread rise in her heart.

She hailed a taxi. "Take me to the bus terminal," she instructed the driver.

It was almost 9 am when Becky walked into the bus terminal and walked over to sit on the stool she had occupied only a few months before. Blanche was ecstatic to see her friend. When the breakfast crowd started leaving, Blanche sat in her old seat, and poured them both a cup of coffee.

Becky leaned forward asking quietly, "Have you heard of The Farm?"

Blanche looked like Becky had slapped her in the face. She whispered demanding, "WHERE did you hear THAT?"

Becky outlined what had happened at the club over the last night. Blanche held a finger to her mouth, hushing Becky.

Blanche ordered Becky her dippy eggs, "Have breakfast, and I'll be finished in a minute. Not Here!" she said under her breath.

Shortly, Becky finished her breakfast. When Blanche's shift ended, the two women went to Blanche's bomb of a car and Blanche drove back to Little Havana.

"One hears things over the years," Blanche started, "but there are times when it isn't healthy to ask questions."

Becky explained how the waitresses above her had been quietly disappearing, and she was being continually promoted.

Blanche stopped at the little park, left the car, and returned to their quiet spot. The two women were away from unwanted ears.

"I've heard of The Farm," Blanche said as she lit a cigarette. Blanche was afraid, Becky could easily tell.

"I've heard that The Farm is a villa somewhere here in Florida, a really high-class place, where girls are taken to be bred."

Becky couldn't believe her ears, "Bred?"

Blanche leaned close; "Rich couples who can't have children of their own, come to town. They see a selection of people in a book, and they can order a breeding, a mating of two people, a male and female."

"NO!" Becky gasped in disbelief.

Blanche nodded her head, "It's Big Business, Becky, BIG MONEY. The couple pays up maybe three hundred thousand dollars or more to get the baby they can't have. There are couples that pay that kind of money. It's BIG BUSINESS. The bred mother is kept at the villa, very much like a resort, very elegant. The female is bred and bred until she can't have any more babies or the demand for her drops."

Becky blinked. She was shaken to the core. "Is that were the girls from the club go, when they aren't seen any more?"

Blanche clutched herself, fearful, "The girls who go to The Farm are the lucky ones. Girls who aren't chosen for The Farm are just sent to the cartel's brothels. Oh yeah, the girls at The Farm are promised they'll be let go, but really when they can't have babies any more, they're just sent to a brothel anyway. They never get out!"

Blanche gasped, "Becky! You have to turn in your two-week notice tonight. I'll negotiate your withdrawal. Once you give Carlos your two-week notice, you're safe. That's your ticket out."

Chapter 6

Later that afternoon the sunlight flooded the apartment as Becky sat in her comfy chair, staring out at the ocean side wall of glass. She could see the beautiful blue water of the Atlantic. A cruise ship ambled by on its way to ports of call in the Caribbean. A high-powered cigarette boat sliced through the water like a hot knife through butter. A fishing boat with its outriggers unfurled started returning to the marina after a full day in the Gulf Stream. The picture was so tranquil.

Becky leaned over and picked up the phone, dialing the number to the El Toro, expecting the desk clerk to answer. She was surprised.

"El Toro, Carlos speaking."

Becky was a little flustered, but managed, "Mr. Hernandez, this is Becky Wolefski. I need to call you to give you my two weeks notice. I want to leave the El Toro and start my own business. Blanche said that if I called and gave an adequate notice, that I could count on a good reference. She said that was a rule of the club."

Becky must have caught Carlos off guard as he covered the mouthpiece. She could hear him talking to someone else. What Becky didn't know was that Carlos was speaking to Raul, "It's Becky, she says she wants to give her notice, and that she would be safe if she did that. Blanche told her it was a rule."

"That's just great, Carlos! I gave you Celeste last night, to teach her how good she had it with me," he looked glaringly at Carlos, who holds up his two ham-hock hands innocently. "So you get her to service you on her knees," Raul recounts, "she scratches you with her teeth, and you cuff her the way you usually hit people, but her head bounced off the pointy corner of the end table, and you kill her. NOW. Celeste's

63

replacement wants to call in and give her notice. Wonderful!" Raul grumped. Carlos stays quiet.

Raul took the phone from Carlos, "Becky," he smiled into the phone, "this is Raaaaul. How can we help you today?"

Becky's eyes widened, "Hello, Mr. Mendoza. I am calling to give the club my two week notice. I want to start a business of my own."

Raul countered, "Yes, Carlos said that. Your call comes at an inconvenient time. Something came up and Celeste had to leave. Carlos and I wanted you to take over her duties at the club. Can I persuade you to change your mind? To stay with us for awhile longer?" he parried.

Becky's heart skipped a beat, "Mr. Mendoza, Blanche said that if I gave my notice, I would be protected and allowed to leave. She said that is A RULE."

Raul paused. Oh how he loved negotiations. It was like a dance. The dip and dive with your partner, moving as one with the samba music. "Yes, yes Becky, Blanche is correct, but I'd like to give you a counter offer," he smiled. "I need you to be the waitress on our flight tonight, one night, and we could consider your two week notice fulfilled. What do you say?"

Becky hesitated, but Raul offered, "I'll throw in four thousand cash for tonight's work. Just to show you that we appreciate your service and loyalty."

'Wow,' Becky thought. That would give me a total of 100,000 dollars total in my bank account to start my company! "Alright, Mr. Mendoza. One flight, one night, and then I'm free?"

"Yes Becky," he grinned, "one flight, one night. That's all I'm asking."

Becky heard herself say, "Ok."

Raul added, "Please take a leisurely bath this afternoon before the flight and relax. I'll have a limousine pick you up at your apartment building at 6 pm sharp. We won't be stopping at the club, so wear your club uniform when we come for you. We'll go directly to the airport from your place."

Becky nodded, "Ok, 6 pm. I'll be ready."

She started to hang up the phone, but changed her mind and dialed another number. Blanche answered. Becky brought Blanche up to date, but seeing the time, cut the conversation short, "but Blanche, it's a lot of money! One flight and I'm out! I'll be ok. You'll see," she said as she hung up the phone.

Becky took a quick hot shower to unwind her tight muscles. She climbed into her black body suit, starched white collar, cuffs, white gloves, and black high heels. She put a trench coat on as she left the apartment door, rode the elevator to the ground floor, leaving the lobby exactly at 6 pm. As promised, the limousine was waiting for her. As she approached, the passenger door opened. She should have guessed, the door was opened by the beast Carlos.

"Come in, Becky," Raul invited.

Seeing the gentleman Raul, Becky stepped into the limousine as the driver closed the door. Immediately, he started the engine and headed toward the airport. Raul and Carlos seemed to ignore Becky, and she was happy that way, although something told her they were following a tight schedule.

At the airport, the limousine went by the passenger terminal, and then turned into the line of corporate hangers at the quiet end of Miami international. Standing in front of a hanger was a gleaming silver twin-engine small private airplane she recognized as a Super G-18.

Long ago, her grandfather had shown her a picture of this corporate airliner circa 1940s. Her grandfather, although a plumber, was also an ardent air enthusiast. He would extol the facts about different airplanes, as he puffed on his ever-present cigar during her stay in Scranton, all those years ago.

Raul, Carlos and she left the stretch limousine, but paused as Raul had a quick word with the pilot as ground crew put three stuffed olive drab duffle bags just inside the airliner's metal door.

"I want to get in the air now," Raul ordered the pilot as he helped Becky into the plane. The pilot made his way to the cockpit and started his final checklist. The interior of the plane was plush, with soft leather chairs lining one side of the plane, with an elaborate bar with stools against the other.

"Better buckle up, Becky," Raul advised, as she heard the deep-throated sound of the port engine begin to whirl, cough into life, then steady down into a smooth spool. Then the starboard engine did the same.

"Miami ground, November niner-niner Whisky requesting permission to taxi, for local VFR flight," the pilot said into the radio. Becky could only hear one side of the conversation.

"November niner-niner Whisky, rog, out," the pilot answered, as the plane's engines surged and the airplane began to roll.

A super G-18 has conventional landing gear, a tail-dragger her grandfather called it, with its nose pointing up. Becky wasn't surprised when they started to fishtail taxi, weaving from side to side as they moved down toward the active runway to take off. The fishtailing movement allows the pilot to see in front of the plane, to make sure there isn't anything in their path as they taxied.

The plane only paused for a moment, then immediately moved onto the active runway, and began its roll to climb into the air. Becky looked outside the window to watch the Miami passenger terminal pass below as the metal giant gained altitude. The plane leveled off once it left the controlled air space around the airport. The sun streamed in the pilot's windshield. They were heading west.

Becky unbuckled and stood up, ready to get Raul his favorite drink, a dark amber special-blended rum on the rocks. When she looked around, she was startled to see Carlos handing Raul his drink, as Raul sat on one of the bar stools.

She was surprised as she looked at Raul, "I thought there would be more people on the flight."

Raul's brilliant white teeth showed as he smiled, "No dear. It's just us. We'll fly west, dropping down to go under the surveillance radar, swing out a little way into the Gulf at five hundred feet, and then turn towards Mobile, Alabama. There we'll file an international flight plan for an over night trip to Bogotá. There is a special auction tomorrow. Rich investors from around the world will attend."

Carlos rested his arms on the bar, patiently waiting. Evidently, this was Raul's show. As usual, Carlos was only the brutal enforcer.

"I don't understand," Becky interjected.

"Of course you don't," Raul cut her off. "We wanted to get to know you a little better, Becky. To establish our union," he grinned.

Becky blinked. She didn't know what to do.

"I have to tell you," Raul continued, "I've been amused watching you these last few months. Celeste has kept me company, and I've not needed any other female companionship." Raul glared at Carlos, who looked down, "but something has come up and Celeste wanted to spend some time in the Everglades, VERY close to the swamp and all its wild animals." Raul looked at Carlos sternly, "I don't believe she'll be rejoining us?" Carlos shook his head no.

Becky protested, "I don't know what you're talking about."

Raul grinned again. He enjoyed this part the most, "The part about you having herpes! That affliction scared away most of the Dons, who would've deflowered you in a heartbeat."

Becky didn't say a word. She just blinked.

"Was the part about you being a virgin true, or like the lie, like you having that sexual disease?" he asked her.

"I am a virgin," Becky answered flatly.

"Oh, that part I can understand," Raul grinned, looking at her over the rim of his drink as he took a long swallow.

"We," Raul pointed to Carlos with a finger from the hand wrapped around his drink, "want to see what's under that body suit. Why don't you take that off so we all can get more comfortable?"

Becky flushed with anger, "I WILL NOT."

Raul raised an eyebrow to Carlos, who started to lumber out from behind the bar. She knew she was going to be stripped naked, whether she cooperated or not.

"Ok! Ok," she answered. Carlos moved from behind the bar and took a seat over by the airplane's door.

Becky slowly unbuckled her collar and cuffs. She took off her gloves.

"Ah, we get down to the important part. Please continue," Raul urged with an evil smile on his face.

Stiffly, Becky unrolled the top of the strapless body suit over her chest and Raul sucked in air. His eyes grew wide with anticipation, "Go on," he urged.

Becky paused. There wasn't any way out. She unrolled the body suit over her athletic hips and let it fall to the floor as she stepped out of it. Except for her black high heels, she stood as the day she was born, but plainly she was a natural and grown woman.

What happened next was maybe for show, but surely for effect. Raul nodded to Carlos who opened and slid the airplane's door into the ceiling. The rush of air through the open doorway while the airplane was still flying was deafening.

"Becky," Raul shouted, " we'll have you tonight, but no one can say I'm unfair. I'll give you a choice. How do you say in this country? Hump or jump?" he grinned questioningly.

As if hit with a bolt of lighting and with the speed of electricity, Becky realized she had to act NOW. She was going TO DIE, sooner or later.

Unexpectedly, she took one step to the doorway and

threw her feet out the door. At the last moment, her right arm shot out, possibly in a final act of desperation, maybe that she didn't want to die. But, as she jumped out the door feet first, her right hand miraculously slid into the shoulder strap on the side of one of the olive drab duffle bags, and instinctively she grabbed the strap for dear-life.

As she jumped from the airplane her body was caught in the engine's slipstream and that force ripped the three stuffed duffle bags out of the plane! Becky fully expected to end her life quickly, but as if by a miracle, or a blessing for her conviction, she hung onto the duffle bags, and she heard a silky "pop" of an opening parachute. Her decent slowed, as the engines from the plane faded.

Carlos raced to the cockpit, "fix that position where we were a minute ago!" he bellowed.

The pilot knew Carlos and immediately did as he was told. Carlos asked, "Where were we?

The pilot looked at Carlos, "We'd just taken off from Miami, traveling west over the everglade swamp. We'd just passed the juncture of the Shark River Slough and Snake Bite Creek. We were directly over Alligator River."

"Call back to Miami, to the company. I want four men, armed and ready, with a helicopter standing by. Get back there NOW," Carlos yelled as the pilot banked the plane, reversing his course.

Alligators are masters at conserving their energy. They float around or lay in wait for their prey to come to them, but sometimes this just isn't possible. Sometimes they have to move toward their dinner. A pair of iridescent eyes snapped open as the heavy throated sound of the twin, piston engine airplane awoke long forgotten instincts. The Everglades are mostly wilderness, a sea of grass, but man is encroaching. Animals need to fight to insure their survival. Darkness was falling. Soon it would be night. An invisible magnet drew the animal forward, silently through the swamp toward where the parachute came down. This basic instinct wouldn't be denied.

Chapter 7

Becky opened her eyes in the predawn half-light, lying on a sandy spit of land jutting into a tidal pool about fifty yards around. She tried to sit up, but almost passed out from an explosion of pain coming from every part of her body, especially her right shoulder and left hip where she landed. She still hugged one of the three duffle bags that had saved her life.

"WHAT have you gotten us into?" Cathy moaned painfully, like when we fell on the ski slope in France three winters ago and broke our leg. "I do what you ask and keep quiet if I can't say anything nice. So what do you do? YOU jump us out of a plane, stark naked, wearing only a pair of stylish black high heels. Wow," she harrumphed, "brilliant."

"Don't start on me, Cathy," Becky tried to sit but couldn't. "It seemed the thing to do at the time. They were going to kill us anyway, just slowly. I decided to get it over as quickly and as painlessly as possible. Fate chose to spare us, why she did, I don't know.

Becky looked around in the growing light. The small point of white-sand beach she was lying on was surrounded in the front and two sides by a green scum-coated pond. On the banks of the pool, she saw dark gray tree logs laying half in and half out of the water. Birds increasingly squawked their various calls from the surrounding jungle in the hellish mangrove swamp, as it got lighter.

Gathering all her might, she managed to sit up. In a minute, her eyes started to focus. She saw that the water under the green scum was brown.

"Becky," Cathy whispered, "Don't look now, but something

71

is moving that green goo around to be able to see that brown water underneath don't ya think?"

'Cathy was right,' Becky thought. She started seeing eyes staring at her in ever increasing numbers. She fearfully saw sets of yellow-green eyes moving closer toward her. She didn't see the pair of blue eyes off to her right.

"WE'RE GONNA DIE," Cathy screamed, but Becky couldn't move.

Becky moved the duffle bag in front of her; trying to protect herself as a huge fourteen foot alligator started lumbering toward her leaving the pool. She took off her high heels in case she had to run, just as the gargantuan alligator lunged at her with an amazing burst of speed, sinking his jaws forcefully into the duffle bag, crushing and ripping it angrily to shreds.

Becky flung her shoes as Cathy screamed, "RUN."

All Becky could do was scoot her butt backward. Her legs wouldn't work.

She didn't at see the younger eight-foot gator slithering out of the pool to her right side until he growled. This was the gator who was going to kill her. He flexed to sprint at her when a hideous beast suddenly broke the surface of the greenish pond, abruptly stood and in two steps flung himself on the younger alligator's back wrestler style, sinking a fourteen inch bowie knife into the gator's spine, pinning him to the beach like a mounted beetle.

Immediately, the pool teemed with movement. All the gators in the pond lunged at the younger alligator that couldn't move, who couldn't defend himself.   "OH MY GOD, BECKY, it's the Reggae Monster from the Black Lagoon!" Cathy screeched.

Becky couldn't believe it! Her heart pounded so hard she thought it would jump out of her chest. That fearsome Monster had saved her!

'I don't know if I should kiss him thanks or scream from

his ugliness,' Becky wondered. Then something absolutely unexpected happened.

Pointing with his arm northward he unemotionally whispered, "Highway 41 is up that-a-way," the monster announced, advising, "you'd better get goin before those croc's finish with him, or they'll eat you next."

Becky blinked, thinking that she was hallucinating. 'Maybe it was the bump on her head?' she wondered.

The feeding frenzy was dying down as the surrounding gators tore off pieces of the young gator, dragging his body parts back into the brown water. The huge human beast with muddy blond dread-locks and a white-blond beard bent down carefully to save his bowie knife from disappearing into the green slime. He wiped the long gleaming blade off on his canvas short shorts; size 32 Cathy guessed, that covered his bare massively muscled thighs. Then he stowed his knife in a scabbard behind his back, hilt pointing to the left. He wore a tan t-shirt, size extra huge; 'maybe 44 inches at the shoulders,' Cathy thought, and had brown canvas high top combat boots. He sported a tan web pistol belt festooned with little pouches and a tie-down type holster with an automatic pistol down his left thigh.

Becky couldn't believe her eyes as she leaned back on her arms in disbelief looking at her guardian angel that spoke English.

"He's a handsome buck, I'll give him that," Cathy interrupted. "He's got to be 6-3, 250 at least, and all muscle. Girl, if I'm going to be marooned in the mangroves with some guy, this is the *stud* for me," she giggled, adding, ',but he's death on two legs,' Cathy admitted cautiously.

Becky's beast didn't say another word. He walked right by her moving toward the jungle, passing her, as if she were just a sack of potatoes! That she was totally naked didn't matter to him one bit. He seemed immune to her charms. "Don't let him get away!" Cathy screeched.

Becky pointed at the alligators that were still gobbling down what was left of the poor young gator; "You can't leave me here with them!"

Without looking back at her, he whispered over his shoulder, "You ain't nothing to me lady," adding, "and I already did my good deed for the day."

"Aren't you curious how I got here? What's in that bag?" she desperately tried to peak his interest.

He was almost in the jungle when she screamed, "STOP, PLEASE stop."

He turned around, looking at her piercingly with ice-cold blue eyes. He took in all of her without batting an eye. Becky felt visually violated, truly naked now.

"Cover yourself honey, your hoo-hoos are showing," Cathy reminded her.

Making a 7 out of her arms, Becky tried to hide herself. She hobbled closer to the only friendly living creature, the only human for miles around.

"I'm lost and need your help! I'm surprised, I'm still alive. I jumped out of a plane last night," she explained.

"If you don't want the highway, lady," the monster went on in his irritating whisper, "just hang around here awhile. The men looking for you and those bags will find you soon. I'm sure they'll help," he offered.

Becky dropped her arms in disbelief, "You saw me jump from the airplane last night?"

"Old habits are hard to break lady," he whispered looking down at her. "For many years I was fed and resupplied by air. The sound of propeller engines and parachutes are like magnets to me, like sounding a dinner bell," he confessed.

Becky's heart stopped, "There are men looking for me?" she gasped.

The monster nodded his head slowly; "Their chopper is searching this way and'll soon be here. If you don't want to meet up with those drug dealers or their hit men, you best go back where you came from."

"I need your help!" she pleaded. "Can't I persuade you somehow?"

"Lady, you're just trouble on two feet, gift-wrapped with pretty brown ribbon. I'm just trying to live my life quietly, away from people. I don't take care of people any more, that ended over a year ago," he told her.

She felt her luck and her energy fail her as she dropped to sit on the sandy beach, drawing her knees to her chin, feet on the ground. She cried, "I don't have any place to go and no one to go home to," she gaspingly sobbed baring her soul. She was at her wit's end, beyond caring what life would do to her anymore.

The filthy beast paused, "What did you say?" he demanded, almost sounding angry. His tone ignited a fire within her.

Becky jumped to her feet and screamed at the top of her lungs, "I don't have anyone to go home to, OK? I'm all alone in life. I've got nothing to live for. Last night I jumped from a plane without a parachute to kill myself. I should have died, but I didn't. JUST MY LUCK. Now I get to be eaten by alligators or sold into white slavery by drug dealers who want to rape me. WOW, what a choice eh? I suppose I couldn't bother you to just shoot me and get it over quick, could I? You look like the mean killer-type, one of those no-feeling, low-life who doesn't care about anyone but himself," she seethed, spraying her spit into his face.

"I don't think you should've done that, Becky," Cathy remarked. He looks like you just slapped him in the face and bloodied his nose. Oh, he looks upset!"

The Monster at first was surprised, then amused by her plucky outburst. He looked away for a moment and mumbled to himself, "Wela said one day I'd have to rejoin the human race. That one day out of the blue, something would change my life, explain to me why I was spared and not allowed to die with my brothers and be at peace. That someone would come into my life that would make my heart beat again. Maybe this is, that day?" He looked at her mumbling to himself again. "As pretty as she is, it's hard to believe no one cares about her, but she is out here in God's country, all alone, and defenseless," he reminded himself. He decided, "I'll go along with her story for now." He looked at her speaking, so she could hear, his tone more civil, "So you don't have anyone to go home to?"

This time it was Becky, who whispered back, her face inches from his, "No, I don't. At least no-one I care to claim," she explained locking her blue eyes to his. Maybe she was mistaken, 'but were his eyes less icy?' she wondered.

He looked at her from out of the corner of his eye, "Well, maybe we can go a little way together," he grumbled, a little less aggressive as he relented a touch.

The giant looked around, "We'd better get outa here if you don't want your buddies catching up with you. I have a camp not far from here. We can go there first," he said turning toward the jungle.

Becky's eyes lit up, "Wait! I have to get my shoes," as she started toward the brush that fringed the clearing. As she neared a bush, rattling sounded.

"STOP," the Monster ordered clearly. Becky froze at his command voice.

The Giant pulled his bowie knife and reached his right hand down by the bush. Instantly, a triangular snakehead with fanged open mouth tried to bite him. He was too fast for the snake, adeptly catching it behind his head. It was like a game to him, like, he'd done it a thousand times. Then with a fast slash of the razor-sharp mini-machete, he severed the snake's head from its body. He nonchalantly threw the head into the jungle fringing the beach.

Becky shivered at the savage sight, at this lethal beast, "I hate snakes."

The monster looked at her, "City girl I guess. You aren't

gonna to last long in this swamp the way you're going. Lucky for you - I happened by," he mumbled as he picked up the snake's body.

She shivered, "You aren't going to keep that, are you?"

"Sure am," he grinned proudly, his white-blond beard nearly hiding his mouth.

Becky gasped, "For a souvenir?"

The giant didn't hesitate, "Heck no, they're good eatin.' They've more meat on 'em than grubs or termites. Not bad in a stew with palm cabbage if you spice 'em good," he mused nonchalantly.

She retched, "You eat grubs and termites?"

Strangely, she was starting a conversation with this Monster from the Black Lagoon. The stranger thing was, that this hideous monster was talking back!

"When I have to," he answered civilly. "I've been a hermit out here. I eat what I can find. Honestly, I like grubs better than termites," he thought, adding, "toasted grubs aren't bad with my horseradish sauce on 'em. They're right tasty. "

Becky felt her stomach start to roll, and she thought she'd throw up. The thought of eating grubs wasn't appealing to her in the least.

He rummaged around in the brush and came up with her shoes, handing them to her, "I think we'd better leave these here. They'll find that torn up bag and your shoes, and think a crocodile got you. Then they'll stop looking and leave us alone."

"Well how am I going to walk around in this hellish jungle and swamp with no shoes on?" she waggled sarcastically.

Her giant turned around, facing away from her, kneeling, presenting his back to her, "Hop on," he invited.

Becky blinked, "Will you please give me your t shirt? I'm stark naked."

The monster flatly whispered, astounding her, "No."

"No," Becky echoed stunned, "Why not?"

"I'm pretty ugly without a shirt lady. You've been scared enough for one day I think," he told her.

"He's pretty dreamy looking from where I'm standin'," Cathy sighed.

"Oh, hush up!" Becky said to Cathy aloud.

"Beg-pardon?" the giant asked, looking at her like, she was crazy.

Becky shrugged shyly, "I talk to myself sometimes. Don't mind me."

The monster saw that Becky's back was starting to burn, even from the little sun that was shining through the surrounding mangrove trees. Reluctantly he pulled his t-shirt over his head in one smooth motion, handing it to her. Her mouth fell open as she took the shirt, unable to take her eyes off his bare torso.

"I told you," the giant frustratingly whispered, reminded her.

"What are all those dimples and slashes all over your chest and sides?" she turned him around, "and your back too? Were you in a war or something?"

The giant's face clouded, "Something like that," he confessed.

He bent down now that Becky happily had his t-shirt on, "Now?" he asked.

Becky scampered on piggyback as her transportation stood up with all her weight, all hundred pounds of her. He wasn't fazed at carrying her in the least. She was like an old familiar feeling, except, she had shaved legs. It was like going home again. He shifted her on his back effortlessly to get comfortable, like, he was rearranging his backpack.

The giant started off at a good pace, covering some distance. He knew where he was headed.

"Where are we going?" Becky asked hanging onto his broad, rock-hard shoulders.

"I stashed my canoe yonder," he pointed out into the open

sea of saw grass. "I'll pole us to where I have my fishing camp," he answered.

"Fishing camp?" she wondered aloud. She didn't see a thing except more little islands of these trees with funny lookin roots that seemed to prop the tree up in the mound of mud or water the tree stood on.

"Yeah, I have a house up north in the Devil's Garden where I'm left alone. The only things up there are me, gators, bugs, and of course snakes. I've been living alone in the Glades for the last year. I was out gathering food when I saw you parachute last night. We don't have grocery stores in the Everglades, which everyone calls The Glades, by the way," he went on. "At least your friends will find their other bag and call off their search, figuring that the crocs got you."

Becky shivered at the thought about the alligators eating her, but then she also sighed, "I worked four months to get enough money to start my own business, but I can't go back to Miami. That's where those men are from. Shame though, I had saved a lot. I guess they'll break open my bank account, siphon it off, and I'll be left where I started."

"At least you're alive," her monster answered. "Here we are," he said as he put her down, uncovering the brush hiding his dugout canoe. It was Indian style, hollowed out from a log with an adze. The canoe was about ten feet long. "Wait a minute," as they both heard a buzzing sound, like an insect inside the canoe.

Carefully, he picked up a long pole from inside the boat and in a scooping motion, flung a snake far into the brush. He smiled, "Pigmy rattler. They're deadly poisonous. He must've crawled in there to take a nap. Almost a shame to bother him," he laughed unaffected. The monster took nature the way she presented it.

Becky saw there weren't any seats in the canoe and in the center was a carefully cushioned military style rifle with scope on the floor of the boat. "My name's Becky, what's yours?" she asked.

He answered, "KIS."

She was a little put off, but gave him a peck on the cheek, "I don't usually kiss on the first date, but you've been sweet so far," she fluffed her hair a bit.

He blinked, and then said, "I'm called KIS, but I appreciate the smooch. I haven't been kissed by a girl before. I guess my size scares girls off. "

"Don't let that go unquestioned girl! Dig for more," Cathy scolded her.

Becky leaned on her other hip, as she looked at this giant of a man a little closer, "You say you haven't been kissed by a girl before? I find that hard to believe."

KIS looked down at her, "I grew up around men lady-er-Becky." He hesitated and strangely seemed to blush, she thought. "I've been kissed by my older sister a time or two, but I don't think that counts being kissed by a real girl," he admitted shyly.

She seemed to swish her hips a little as he helped her into the boat. He didn't see the smile that lurked at the corner of her lips, nor the twinkle in her eye.

KIS helped her kneel on some rags in the front of the canoe. He got in, pushing them out into the center of a small rivulet. He remained standing as he poled the canoe down the small trail of water in traditional Indian style.

"Where are we?" she asked looking around.

"We're near Alligator Bay, some call it Whitewater Bay, on the west coast of Florida, almost at the ocean, in the Glades," he told her

At the mention of gator, Becky jumped, "Are there alligators close by?"

"When I found you, those were crocodiles really," he seemed to lecture her. "We're in the middle of the dry season. The fresh water is pulling back and the salt water from the

Gulf is coming into these mangrove swamps. The water's too salty for alligators to live in now. Adult crocodiles can live in salt water. Alligators are fresh water animals. Alligators are all around the Glades. Almost everything in the Glades bites or is poisonous," he stated a fact.

To Becky, crocodiles or alligators, both were the same. They both represented a hideous death that walked on four legs.

Becky looked at the strange trees with legs standing in the mud of some of the little islands that dotted the grassy plains, "What are those trees?"

"They're mangrove trees," he told her. "There're three kinds of mangrove, red, white, and black. The mangrove tree is the only tree that can live in salt water."

She started feeling sick to her stomach. Almost being killed several times, jumping from the airplane; nearly being eaten by the crocodile was getting the better of her. KIS saw it right off. He poled over to one of the little islands and plucked several leaves from a tree, handing it to her, "Lick the leaves," he said.

Reluctantly she did as he told her, and she was amazed at the salty taste. He grinned, "You're running low on electrolytes and the salt from the black mangrove leaves will make you feel better. The mangrove tree makes fresh water from the salt water, excreting the salt on its leaves."

Suddenly, he leaned down and picked something off the mangrove tree. He took a metal coffee can from inside the boat, scooped some salt water from the rivulet and dropped the shell into the salt water. He looked into the can for a few minutes then reached in and took out the shell. He took a rock from inside the canoe and broke the small, conk-like shell, picked out the meat, offered some to Becky who amazed, watched this monster have a light snack.

All of this was so strange to Becky. KIS answered her questioning look, "Mangrove crab," he explained. "Crabs live on the mangrove trees and eat parasitic bugs and algae that grow on the tree, in a symbiotic relationship. If you put them in water, they drown. Then you can easily break the shell, and they're mighty good if you don't mind them wiggling goin down," he grinned.

In another thought KIS added as he pointed to the clear water near the roots of the mangrove trees. Becky saw hundreds of little minnows, tiny fish swimming about, "Over half the world's fish population begins its life in mangrove swamps both north and south of the equator in what's called the Mangrove Belt. Astronauts can see this green mangrove vegetation from space. It's really amazing the wealth of nature and the benefit the Everglades Swamp brings to the entire world. If only more people knew how precious she was to us all here on earth," he confessed. "People shouldn't try to drain the water from the Glades." I think all of us on this planet need to learn to live together in peace with nature as well as other people. That's our only hope of survival."

KIS paused, "There's one of those bags," he pointed out, floating under a branch of a tree at the edge of the rivulet.

"Go back. Go back PLEASE!" Becky urged.

"Becky, if we leave the bag, they'll find it eventually, and it'll all be over. We can live our lives in peace. The Glades is my home. I live here. If we take that bag, we're gonna have to kill people and eventually leave," he stated flatly. "Are you willing to kill people over that bag? Is the money worth both our lives?"

Becky thought long and hard. She thought about all that had happened, "Yes, I'm willing to kill. I'm fed up. I'm going to start fighting back. I'm tired of being the little girl, being pushed around by macho bullies."

KIS thought about that was going on, that he was getting in deeper with this stranger. Did he want to sign on with all her troubles? Did he really believe she was alone in life?

"How much do you think is in the bag?" he asked.

Becky opened the duffle and carefully counted the packs of one hundred dollar bills, "A million dollars," she answered firmly. "We'll split it 50-50 if you help me."

He thought for a minute then looked at her, "I've killed for my country for many years for a lot less money. A tribe of Indians adopted me when I had no one to care for me. They need help now, financial and legal, to keep their lands and homes. I'll help you in order to help them. I have to warn you though, we might have a short but illustrious life."

He poled their canoe from the rivulet out into a long stretch of open water as the three foot saw grass waved with the gentle breeze, "We're at the end of the dry season and most things are either dead or hibernating. As summer comes on and the rains start in early June, life will renew itself in the glades," he told her.

She smiled, listening to him, "You love it here don't you? You talk about this place with such passion, with considerable knowledge. I'm impressed."

Before she got her reply, KIS crouched down partially. He seemed to hear something she didn't. Quickly, expertly he poled to get their canoe back in the rivulet, hiding, just as she heard the sound of an engine coming closer.

"What is it," she whispered,

KIS's eyebrows frowned, "An airboat. It's how we get around in the Glades fast. There aren't fishermen out this time of year, so I'd say whoever's in the boat are probably your friends."

"You mean drug men?" she wondered aloud.

"I'd say hit men, or at least a clean-up crew," KIS whispered back. "Those guys were out here last night in a chopper and found one of the bags hangin from a branch way out over the water. Some Ya-hoo got the bright idea to lower one of the men down on a steel cable to get the bag, but he couldn't reach it on the line, so he unhooked himself, attached the bag to the cable, but before he could attach the cable to himself again, he fell into the water. He started splashing and thrashing about in the water. Man, that's the last thing you wanna do in the Glades. Alligators or crocodiles are attracted to sound and scent. They can't see very well."

"And the crocs got the man in the water," Becky cringed, finishing the story?

"Yup," KIS replied curtly, and then offered, "I could just pop these guys a third eye real quick from this distance, and save ourselves a whole lot of trouble."

"You mean to kill them outright? Murder them?" she gasped.

KIS nodded his head, "If we let them get close, it can get dangerous, not to mention bloody."

Becky was cut off, as the airboat got closer, then slowed. Her hesitation had made the decision for them. Though their canoe was hidden, the airboat idled as it neared the juncture of their rivulet and the long main stream.

"Why you stoppin, man?" they heard a man in the boat ask.

"I thought I saw mud, coming from that rivulet. Like a boat had just passed," the man piloting the airboat answered. "Look down that little stream," but he stopped talking as KIS started poling their canoe towards the men.

"If shootin starts, stay low," he whispered to Becky, "I'm gonna be shooting over you from back here."

"Hello! What's up gentlemen?" KIS demanded confidently as he pointed the canoe at the drifting airboat, the propeller stopped so they could talk.

One man on the flat of the boat stood up, his arms moving towards machine pistols hanging on each side of his body. Becky didn't move, but heard KIS unsnap the strap over his pistol as he talked.

"We were out fishin, my woman and I," KIS called to the men in the boat.

The driver of the airboat sat forward and smiled, "Amigo,

I think you don't speak the truth. I think your woman is the girl we are searching for. Our boss has unfinished business with her," he wickedly grinned adding, "not to mention she has mucho money of hes."

Becky's heart thumped in her chest. Would KIS give her over to these drug men to save himself?

The two boats were about twenty yards apart now, drifting in the breezy current. They were at a standoff.

"Give us the girl, amigo, and we let you go," the man standing in the bottom of the boat offered, seeming to be the crew leader. The other two men in the boat weren't that anxious to get into a fight. It was the man standing with the twin mak-10s who seemed ready to tussle. KIS spoke mainly to him, but kept his eyes on the other two.

"Friend, you're humpin the wrong man's leg. I say YOU turn around and leave us alone, or YOU are gonna DIE," KIS answered, with a strange anger tone in his voice.

When the man in the front of the boat translated what KIS had just said into Spanish in his head, so that he understood the insult completely, he jerked, drawing the twin pistols up, but KIS had anticipated his move. KIS drew his automatic pistol and Becky strangely saw a third red eye appear, just as the man fell backward into the water. KIS shot the other two men in the head also, like one, two, three.

Becky almost passed out, realizing that her giant had just expertly shot three men dead who were bristling with weapons. He was out-gunned three to one!

"Guess these gangsters tried to hump the wrong man's leg," Cathy cackled.

Chapter 8

A cloud of gun smoke drifted in the air while the shock waves of the staccato shots faded. This was a new experience for Becky. Visible violence hadn't been part of her social calendar either back in Chicago or recently in Miami. She'd been protected from the raw side of life. Her life was unprotected now, but KIS was helping her navigate the stormy part of her new existence.

KIS didn't waste time and poled the canoe right beside the floating airboat. "Get in," he told Becky, still shaken by the abrupt bloodshed. He helped her step into the twenty-one foot airboat, having a flat bottom with blunt but curved-up bow, and two tandem-elevated driver seats, in front of the engine and airplane propeller.

Once she was safely aboard, KIS got in the airboat also, quickly tied the canoe to the airboat's gunnel cleats and then immediately went to the side of the boat where the twin pistolero fell overboard. 'Yup,' just where he thought he'd be. KIS leaned down over the side, grabbed the floating man and stripped the leather harness off him. The two machine pistols with their long one hundred round magazines protruded from the bottom of the pistol handles.

KIS tried on the harness, "Not bad," he smiled, pleased with himself.

KIS was looking around the boat, "Great, they smoke my brand!" he exclaimed in a hushed tone as he uncovered a wooden crate with 9mm stenciled in black on the top. He checked the magazines in the machine pistols, though he knew they were fully loaded. The would-be bad man didn't even get off a shot before his well-placed bullet to the forehead ended his days.

KIS found canvas travel bags under the seat. There he saw what he was looking for. He took out a clean shirt from the bag and held it up in front of Becky checking the fit, "Try this one," he told her, "it seems clean."

She tried the shirt on as KIS pulled out a fresh pair of jeans, looking from the pants to her hips, "No, too small," he decided.

"Why don't you let me see what fits, since it seems you want to dress me from extra clothes in this bag," She stated. "Go do what you need to do."

KIS nodded thinking, 'she seems like a level-headed girl,' he grinned. 'Not bad for being in her first firefight and not curled up in the corner like a sissy.'

A big splash from the side where the first bandit had been floating caught both KIS and Becky's attention, "What was that?" she gasped.

"Croc got him," KIS explained. "Croc's are like the cleanup crew of the swamp. When they're hungry, they'll eat most anything, even themselves."

Aghast for a moment, Becky thawed and continued searching the bags for garments that would fit. She realized KIS was trying to get her comfortable in clean clothes where he could, as there certainly weren't any department stores near the Pa-hay-okee Overlook section in the Everglades. She found a pair of jeans and tried them on. 'Great in the seat, but too long,' she thought to herself.

KIS saw her dilemma. He took out his ever-present bowie knife, "Stand up, tell me how long you want the legs to be. I'll hem them for you."

Becky laughed, "don't tell me you're a tailor too among your ever-growing number of talents?"

KIS smiled broadly, "I'm a man of many skills," he whispered then returned to her pant legs and rolled them up to where she nodded. He had her sit on the lower seat in the boat, rolled the pant legs down about an inch from where she wanted them hemmed, pushed the razor-sharp blade in the legs and trimmed off the excess cloth. Then he took a fishing line and suture needle from one of the pouches on his pistol belt, and efficiently hemmed the pant leg.

"Stand up," he told her.

"Oh that's wonderful!" she said surprised, "Where'd you learn to sew?"

KIS looked at her, "When I got to Boot Camp and we got our first issue of clothes, the DI – er Drill Instructor divided us up in pairs. It was a teamwork exercise. One guy hemmed the other guy's pants, then they traded places."

KIS reached into one of the other pouches on his pistol belt and took out a plastic bag containing some light brown colored cigars. Looking at her, "Do you mind if I smoke?"

"Go ahead KIS. You've earned it. I've come to enjoy the smell of a good cigar," she told him.

"I try to buy hand rolled cigars when I can. I like Dominican with a Connecticut wrapper myself. It's a mild combination, but rich in taste. It's my one vice," he smiled, taking a gadget from another pouch, putting a hole in the rolled end of the cigar for the smoke to come through. Taking out a butane lighter, he carefully warmed the tobacco then puffed the cigar to life.

Becky was noticing KIS was slowly opening up little by little. She saw he wasn't a gabber-mouth by any means. He was very much like the studly guards at the El Toro, very capable, but governed by some code of honor.

Now that her pants were hemmed, he went about scavenging any useable items and dumping the other two dead men over the side as they were starting to stink. She found a pair of sneakers in one of the bags that reasonably fit. She was glad at least that one of the hit men was near her size.

She didn't look as the dead men disappeared beneath the brownish water of the main channel with splashes and guttural growls. Their bodies proved to be nourishing for the growing number of crocs close to the boat.

KIS rummaged through the bags, making sure; there wasn't anything in them that could give their position away. Then he dumped them overboard and sunk them with a pole, preparing to get underway.

"Where to next?" she asked her husky companion. "Which boat are we going to take?"

KIS looked around, it was nearing noon, judging by the sun overhead. Suddenly, their peace was shattered by the sound of a radio laying on the driver's seat.

"Julio, where are you?" the radio crackled.

KIS scanned the horizon. His fear was confirmed.

"We've got to get outa here," as KIS pointed to the east.

Becky's eyes followed his arm, and she saw a lone chopper flying a search pattern low over the Glades. Her pulse quickened for another reason.

"I know that voice!" she breathed anxiously.

KIS grabbed the radio and moved toward his canoe. He helped her back into the tiny boat.

"I want to get away from this airboat. To use it for bait," he said as he pushed off and started to pole down the canal, looking for something.

Becky didn't know what her protector was looking for, but she was starting to trust his judgment. He'd saved her life several times today. Strangely, she was feeling something budding within her, something she hadn't ever felt before.

KIS found a dimple in the wall of saw grass and mud, almost imperceptible to the untrained eye. He nosed the boat into the gator slide in the bank of the main stream, stepping over her to beach the canoe. In a minute, he reappeared from the brush, "Come on. I've got an idea," he told her.

"What is this?" Becky asked.

"It's a gator trail running back into the saw grass. Gators use this to get from their nests to the channels of water close to their lairs," KIS explained. "At the start of the wet season, gators mate, then the female goes back into the grassy prairie to make her nest. She first digs a shallow hole in the mud, lays her eggs, then covers the eggs with leaves and grass, then covers that with more mud. The decomposing leaves make heat and acts as a natural incubator for her eggs, so she doesn't have to sit on the nest like birds do."

Becky froze, "You mean there are gators close by? This is their street, in the mud?"

KIS took Becky's tiny hand in his massive paw, "Come-on, we'll be ok. If we meet a gator he'll be as surprised to see us, as we are to see him."

Becky froze. KIS stopped, "Don't worry. I'll take care of you. If we meet an alligator I'll make a handbag out of him for you." He patted his bowie knife, "I speak their language." Then KIS uncommonly looked worried as he scanned the moist ground, "What I'm worried about is fire ants. They're hard to see and can sting the heck out of you. Fire ants and gator nests are a usual combo."

"Oh great," she muttered under her breath as she walked bent over under the canopy of waving saw grass.

The mud of the bank smelled retched and moldy. She wrinkled her nose against the stench, but her heart raced from the sound of the approaching copter.

KIS pulled the canoe under the waving saw grass that camouflaged it. She was sure their position couldn't be seen from above.

He pulled out a pair of powerful binoculars handing them to Becky, "Can you see the helicopter? Do you recognize any of the men inside?" he asked.

He showed her the focusing knob. She moved it until the helicopter's cabin became visible.

"Yes, the man with the pony-tail, sitting on the left. He's one of the bad men, one of those who are chasing me. He's

Carlos Hernandez," her heart skipped a beat. He's a monster, a killer," she explained.

KIS, stone-faced took up his rifle with a telescopic sight, peered through it at the helicopter. Seeing the man Becky pointed out, "Is he one of the men who would hurt you?" he asked.

She nodded, "He's very bad, an enforcer in the drug gang. He's one of the men I tried to get away from when I jumped out of the airplane last night."

KIS looked at Becky and then back through his scope, made an adjustment on it, then waited for a situation or something, she wasn't sure. She held her breath. She didn't know what would happen next.

The helicopter must've spotted the airboat floating in the main channel. The chopper turned and started approaching straight on as he and Becky kneeled in the mud in a small opening in the sea of saw grass.

KIS saw that there were three men in the chopper, the pilot, the man with the ponytail, and a door gunner. 'Pretty standard,' he thought.

Becky looked through the binoculars. Staring at her tormentor, Carlos.

KIS's rifle erupted loudly, followed quickly by two more reports. Three shots were fired and executed with deadly accuracy.

Becky saw the windshield of the chopper in front of Carlos shatter as Carlos was thrown back into his seat, then his head snapped limply forward as his chest blossomed scarlet red. The other two shots shattered the windshield in front of the pilot and then immediately the door gunner sagged limp as a rag doll. The chopper did an unceremonious nose-dive into the field of saw grass. A massive yellow-orange explosion erupted as the rotors contacted the grassy field, spraying burning gasoline, mud, and pieces of chopper everywhere.

"Are they all dead?" Becky looked at KIS, her heart racing wildly.

He stood up in plain sight now, "I certainly hope so," he stated flatly. "When Kyle puts the KIS of Death on somebody, he expects them to stay dead."

This was such a macabre world. She wasn't used to all the violence. She woozily shook her head, and vomited. In a minute she asked, "Who's Kyle?"

KIS gently laid his rifle in the bottom of the canoe, careful that the scope wasn't jarred and was secure to move about. Next, he helped Becky wobble over and take her familiar spot in the front of the boat, as he pushed off, poling over to the airboat once again.

"That's me, Kyle Ibsen Swoboda, at your service Ma'am," he smiled. I'm a dealer in death. Violence is my middle name."

Becky turned her head around to look at this strange man who was constantly amazing her, "Whaa?" she groaned.

"I know," he grinned amused, "I have that effect on people. I leave them speechless or dead," he laughed in his constant whisper.

As they neared the airboat, she burped up, "You just killed three MORE people! Doesn't your killing them bother you at all?"

Unaffected he countered, "You said that first hombre was a bad man."

"And he was," she answered carefully, "He killed one of my friends."

"Just my point," KIS established, "so then he deserved to die."

She turned around at the waist, "But what about the pilot and the man in the doorway. I don't know about them. They could've been innocent.

Confidently KIS answered her, "They were guilty by association. No one made that pilot fly for them. That guy in the doorway was what we call – a door gunner, so I say he was a threat. I don't see the problem. I just cleaned three dangerous men from society. I figure it was a good day's work."

"Won't the authorities start getting involved, or are they used to your homicidal tendencies?" she wondered aloud rolling her eyes.

KIS pulled up alongside the airboat, held it steady, nodding his head yes, he wanted her to get in, which she did. KIS threw his possible bag into the airboat, taking hold of his rifle; he got in, and made a careful bed for his rifle with life preservers on the bottom of the airboat.

"I know the Sheriff of these parts. Sheriff Mo the local's call him. We sometimes go fishin and we've gone huntin a time or two. He knows my skills. He was in the Corp aways back, like many police officers are," KIS explained.

"You mean the Sheriff knows you kill people?" she asked incredulous.

KIS smiled, "The gang violence of Miami is starting to flow over into the Glades. The Sheriff is a reasonable man. As long as the gang violence doesn't come into his town and hurt someone he knows, he doesn't get upset if some bad men disappear, which they usually do out here," he explained.

"Disappear?" she gasped.

KIS waved his hand toward the hit men who were eaten by the crocodiles, "Disappear, as if never heard of again, kind of dis-appear."

This was the first time KIS could get a really good look at the boat, "Oh Man!" he exclaimed aloud.

Becky hadn't heard much emotion from the strange monster, so his excitement caught her attention, "What?"

KIS explained, "This is one of those long distance drug-running airboats I've seen whizzing around the Glades at night. Drug dealers from Miami run across the Glades picking up drug drops near the Gulf and run back to Miami in the same night. She's a beauty!" He pointed the boats features out to

Becky, "She has two pilot seats, one in front of the other each with a rudder pole and accelerator pedal, and probably a 454 cubic inch V-8 engine, a four-barrel carburetor with blower, with one eight-foot wooden prop in a good metal fence guard cage. OH MAN, this baby is sleek and FINE. She's built to ride all night!"

Becky couldn't help herself, "Why do men call machines by feminine names? It sounds sexist to me. I never understood that."

KIS stopped, "An old Gunny told me once that if you treat machines like a beautiful lady, with respect and care, she will take care of you when you need her help. I guess it is just old school."

KIS found what he was looking for along each side of the boat, "We've got twin twenty-three gallon gas tanks!" he grinned. Looking inside each, "The port tank is full, but the starboard tank is almost empty. These guys must've been a good distance from their last fuel stop and far from their home base." Kiss looked a little sheepish, "I probably shouldn't have lit the cigar with all this gasoline on board, but I like to have a smoke after I do the deed. It's my trademark," he grinned unashamed.

Becky blinked. She understood he could have blown them up if the gasoline had ignited.

KIS squared his shoulders at her, "I told you we might have a short, but illustrious life.

Becky looked at KIS and then ignored the thought asking, "What's port and starboard? You lost me with that stuff."

KIS didn't look up as he was preparing to get underway, "Port is a naval term for left and starboard is right."

A dark cloud crossed his face, "We'd better di di mao. I don't fancy running into any more of their buddies. Believe it or not, I'm getting tired of killing people. I must be getting soft and out of practice, getting soft!" he confessed.

She blinked, and then asked, "What's di di mao?"

He climbed up into the pilot's seat. He reached his hand down, which she grabbed trusting her guardian angel, and she was hauled up to sit in the seat behind him, as if she were as light as a feather.

'OH, maybe he'll let me drive a little,' she thought to herself. Once in the seat she had to lean forward so she could hear him. He reached down beside the pilot's seat, and pushed the starter button on a control panel. The propeller twirled behind them and the engine sputtered to life. The noise was deafening.

"Di di mao is Viet Namese for lets-get-outa here," he shouted over the roar of the engine. He depressed the gas pedal and the engine accelerated. The pole on their left controlled the rudder, the gizmo that steered the airboat she saw.

KIS was like a kid with a new toy. Driving the airboat was pretty much like flying a plane. He could control the airboat expertly, something that didn't miss her attention. He seemed good at all he did. He was extremely talented.

She went back to what they had been talking about a little while ago, "You were talking about the gas in the tanks. What about them?"

KIS grinned; "This boat has big gas tanks."

She looked at him with a bland stare, "Y-eah. Is this a guy-thing? You know, who has the bigger one?"

KIS grinned broadly, "No, but the size of the gas tanks means how far we can go before we have to stop and refuel. No gas, no motor. It's very simple."

She dropped her head, "OK, I'm game. How far can we go?"

KIS stopped and thought for a minute. He was calculating something.

"I figure we can travel at least four hours on each tank, going flat out, but that's not how we travel in the Glades. Everything is piece-meal, very zigzag," he explained. "We are in the dry season so some of the flat lands are dry, some are wet. This airboat has a shallow draft, means we don't go deep into the water. We can skim over any land or mud that has the slightest covering of water. Mostly, we'll stick to the canals or rivulets," he told her.

She could see this. The canals aren't straight, they're like highways that dip and dive around natural barriers.

"Do we have enough gas to get to where we need to go?" she asked.

"No, I don't think so, not enough to get to my home at least. We're north of Mahogany Hammock, west of Pa-hay-okee Overlook. We want to get to my house up in the Devil's Garden. We need to go up to the Rookery Branch of the Shark River Slough, head northeast, up to Hardwood Hammock, and then we'll soon be home. I know a fishing village along the way we can stop and gas up. That's about three quarters way to my house," he answered, in plain English.

KIS made a quick detour to his fishing camp to pick up his belongings. He stopped long enough to break down his one-man tent, grab his pack, fishing poles, and tackle box. They'd already decided where they were going. He didn't want to linger in this neck of the swamp in case any more choppers were near by. He jumped back into the airboat, restarted the engine and gunned her into the nearest main channel. They headed northeast again at full throttle.

"Do you live in a town?" she asked.

They were whizzing down the main channel cranking out thirty miles per hour, working their way through the fields of three-foot saw grass via bordering canals. She saw how he looked up ahead to pick the canal that traveled roughly the way they wanted to go. If there wasn't a canal, KIS would skim the airboat anywhere there was even an inch of water, just enough to let the boat slide over the lily pads.

"I live on an island actually," he answered, but didn't say more. In a little while he told her, "Once we get over the horizon from the chopper, I want you to learn how to drive this boat. Never know when it might come in handy for you to be able to pilot one of these airboats."

"ME?" she thrilled, wanting to try it!

"I'm ex-military," he told her. "These are the 90's and women do many things these days. I don't mind as long as we don't step on each other's toes. I believe in good communication, close contact," he emphasized.

"OH, I so get that," she hummed to herself.

Chapter 9

As soon as they were over the horizon, KIS traded seats with Becky and instructed her on how to drive the airboat. It took a little while for her to get used to coordinating the controls. Driving an airboat is a combination of flying an airplane, piloting a boat, and driving a car. The left-hand stick controls the rudders that move the airboat from side to side and the gas pedal on the floor controls the propeller, which controls the forward motion. Like a boat though, an airboat doesn't have any brakes. Becky was surprised that KIS was such a good teacher. He was very patient with her, stayed close to her as she was learning, but he gave her space to learn on her own.

"You're doing great, Becky," he encouraged her.

She squealed, "OH, this is so much fun! And to think I don't even drive a car," she laughed as the wind played with her hair.

KIS liked seeing her have fun. He enjoyed the sound of her laugh.

After awhile, she turned around, "I'd better let you take over if we're going to get where we need to be, before nightfall. Can we do this again sometime?"

KIS got back into the pilot's seat and took over the controls, settling into a ground covering pace, "Sure can," he told her. "Maybe we can take a day out and go for a picnic."

"OH, I'd love that," but she added a little anxious, "Is there a place you know of around here where there're no snakes or alligators?"

KIS twisted his face, deep in thought, "I'm not sure there is in the swamp. Wild animals are everywhere here, but you get used to it. It's a shame; civilization is encroaching on the Everglades. Developers want to drain the land, so they can build more homes. Farmers want to divert the natural water that is the lifeblood of The Glades to irrigate their crops," he told her, "which would kill the vegetation and all the animals who live in this wilderness. There are wading birds that depend on the shallow water to feed, many species use the shallow water to hatch their eggs and let their babies grow to adulthood to enter the food chain. "What's crazy, he said, "is that most of Florida is only fourteen feet above sea level, could easily go underwater if there were a huge storm serge, and hurricanes are common in this location. Nature depends on natural disasters like hurricanes and devastating fires regularly to renew herself. This swamp ISN'T meant to be domesticated," he explained. "People have tried to farm this land, but found that was a mistake. Nature will fight back against civilization."

"Wow," Becky exhaled. I never knew about this place until now.

The airboat traveled over the marshland, using the rivulets, zigzagging around mangrove islands and natural barriers. The land was mostly flat like the prairie, with waving fields of yellow grasses and scrub trees here and there.

Three hours passed. Becky's bottom was going numb from the vibration of the boat's engine just behind her and was ready for a stretch. A small fishing village appeared along the canal up ahead on the right. KIS maneuvered the airboat alongside the wooden dock that had seen many seasons. A black-haired young man, in his late teens caught the rope KIS tossed to him.

"Hey, Pima," KIS shouted, "Good to see you again."

The young boy stood up and stretched, "Home is the Great Hunter KIS, home is the murderer and liar!"

'WOW', Becky thought, 'That wasn't a very pleasant welcome! Not what I would've expected. I thought KIS was liked by the people here-about,' fearfully she realized, 'I guess NOT'.

"Good to see you too, Pima. How've you been Bro?" KIS tried again.

Pima looked angrily at KIS, "I'm not YOUR BRO, KIS. You might've fooled Osola with your white-man tricks. He mistakenly took you as his blood brother, but you're not my brother. I'd rather cut my arm off first," he retorted and stomped off.

Becky stood stock still as KIS moved the boat close to the gas pump and started filling the boat's tanks. They were nearly dry.

"Geez," I didn't expect that KIS," she mentioned, a little worried.

KIS continued fueling the boat, "I should've expected that from Pima, but I'd hoped his anger had lessened over the last year. I've kept away from this place for some time now."

He finished putting fuel in the tanks, "I'm gonna go pay. Stay close to the boat. You'll be ok. I won't be long."

"OK, I'll be right here. It's good to be on land again, standing on something that isn't moving," she answered. She threw his t-shirt, "Here, you better put this on," he caught it as he walked away.

She watched her dread-locked, bearded monster walk down the pier and up into the village on land off to the right. She was left alone with her thoughts and the gentle lapping sound of water as it kissed the pilings of the pier.

An older woman with a touch of gray in her long black hair walked toward Becky, holding a wooden box and some letters, "Where's KIS?" she asked Becky looking around. "Pima said he came in. I have his cigars and mail."

Becky's heart skipped a beat, "Are you KIS's wife?" she stammered.

The older woman looked at Becky as if for the first time, "No, NO," she answered half laughing-half serious as she realized the question.

Becky relaxed a bit; glad she wasn't stealing another

woman's man. "I don't know KIS very well. We just met actually," she shrugged.

"I'm Wela, KIS's older-widowed-blood-sister. I know that's a mouthful. KIS and my younger brother Osola, became blood brothers, so KIS is a member of our tribe," she explained.

Becky gave a cautious single nod with her head, "Ah, that explains part of it at least. My name's Becky."

Wela looked at the girl, "Ok Becky, why don't you come with me, and we can have a cup of tea? It'd be lovely to get to know you." Wela saw Becky's concern, "Don't you worry your head, girl. KIS has his eye on you all the time. Matter-o-fact, you're the first girl he's ever brought here, and probably you're the first girl he's been alone with in his entire life. You must be VERY special."

Becky laughed, "I thought that part about him not being kissed by a girl before, after I kissed him, other than by his older sister was just a joke."

Wela stopped dead in her tracks, "You kissed him? He let you?"

Becky blushed, "All I did was kiss him on the cheek. Honest! We didn't do more than that," she said hesitantly. She was afraid Wela would be angry thinking, she'd let her brother fool around with her when they were alone in the swamp. Some people in the back country can be very protective of their relatives. Becky was afraid Wela would be offended she'd kissed her brother.

Wela put her hand over her heart, "By the Spirits' girl, maybe you're the savior? I've prayed this whole last year for someone to bring my brother back from the land of the dead. I'd about given up hope! He wouldn't even look at any girls I tried to introduce him to. Look at him. He's let himself go and turned into a dirty hermit." Wela stopped in front of a chickee, a house on stilts about three feet off the ground with a thatched, palmetto-palm leaf roof.

The interior of the house wasn't large, but was divided

into a kitchen, living space and a bedroom. It was neat and immaculately clean. Wela walked into the kitchen and put a kettle on a small two-burner propane stove. She took out two modest cups and tea bags.

"My brother Osola, KIS called him Owl, met in Boot Camp. They were Marines together and were very close. They were in several battles together," Wela explained further.

The kettle started screaming. Wela poured hot water in both cups offering cream from a condensed milk can on the counter and sugar cubes from a small bowl. Once they fixed their tea, Wela led the way to the small couch in the living room.

"The men were going to get out of the Marines after their last leave down here," Wela went on. "They were going to start a business together. Osola was going to raise alligators and KIS is a pilot, so he was going to fly fisherman around, or take them in an airboat to special fishing places here in the Glades."

Becky sat forward, "I was wondering about KIS. He seems so mechanically inclined."

Wela smiled, "Oh yes, KIS is good with his hands."

Becky stiffened a little, but Wela was quick to add, "Oh no. Not in the way you're thinking. KIS isn't like that at all! He almost has his mechanical engineering degree, along with having a commercial pilot's license already. What I meant about being good with his hands is that he can fix anything mechanical. He loves engines of any kind. Engines seem to sing to KIS's heart. He lights up with excitement over machines. It's a little strange, but everyone is different. Everyone has a different purpose here on Mother Earth."

Becky felt relieved, "So that part of him, never being with a girl is true?"

Wela leaned a little closer, "Yes dear. You're the first girl I know of whose kissed him. He's an unplucked flower," she giggled. "From what Osola told me, he didn't know much how a girl was made, since he grew up around men on a farm up north in Pennsylvania. They're pretty religious up there," she added.

Becky surprised asked, "Pennsylvania? OH, do you know where in Pa?"

"He was born in a place called Sunbury, but he's an orphan and grew up on his uncle's farm in Lancaster County, I think. Do you know it?" Wela asked.

A smile crossed Becky's lips, sitting a little straighter, "Oh yes, it isn't far from my grandparents' home in Scranton. It's not really close, but not too far either, if you know what I mean." Wela nodded. She understood.

Becky urged, "So why didn't the guys get out of the Marines? Where's Owl, I mean Osola? OH!" she cringed, "he isn't dead, is he?"

Wela fidgeted with a white lace handkerchief, "Yes, Osola has gone to the Great Spirit and is with the other warriors of our tribe. The men were going to turn in their discharge papers, but when they got back to the base, the First Gulf War in Kuwait had started. The boys were frozen in the service of our country."

Dabbing the corner of her eye with the handkerchief Wela added, "I made Osola promise to bring KIS back alive as I made KIS promise the same thing, for KIS to bring Osola back to me too. One of my brother's came home alive, I think. The other brother came back to me, in a box," she gaspingly sobbed.

When Wela got hold of herself, Becky was desperate to learn more. She gently urged, "Go on please? What happened?"

"They were in the Air War Portion of Operation Desert Storm, in the Kuwait Desert, it was February 1992. On their last mission, they'd been in the freezing winter desert in Kuwait for over three weeks. Osola was KIS's spotter. KIS was a sniper and a darn good one too," she emphasized. "The men in KIS's squad were all killed and so was Osola, protecting KIS, taking the bullets meant for him. It was an accident that the enemy discovered them. I won't see the physical form of Osola in this lifetime, but I know my brother is with me in spirit. I feel his presence."

"OH MY GOD," Becky exhaled. "That explains a lot Wela. I know it was hard to tell what happened, but KIS doesn't say much. I guess most combat veterans are that way when they come home. I remember my grandpa was in the Second World War and was in Europe. He and I would talk about him being in the Army and in the war. He'd talk about his experiences, but he was very guarded, very careful about the fighting and those who died in battle."

Wela added, "The thing you need to remember Becky, about KIS, is that he and Owl were behind the lines Marines, snipers. The men sometimes would have whole conversations with hand signals alone, using sign language. Snipers are silent men. Sound could give their position away and that could kill them. They don't often talk above a whisper," she shared this secret with Becky.

Becky realized the time, "I'd better be getting back. KIS won't know where I've gone."

Wela smiled, "You like him, don't you?"

Becky tried to put it into words; "He's done more for me in a day than any male ever has. I feel safe with him, and there's something more ..."

Wela smiled, "I understand. It's important for a woman to feel safe with the man she has chosen. It's been this way with women throughout history."

Becky blinked, but didn't respond. Maybe she wasn't ready to have that conversation with herself, yet.

The two women walked down the dirt path back to the canal. Becky saw a tall, giant man with his dread-locks and beard. He was unmistakable.

As the two women approached KIS, Wela continued forward and kissed him on his beard, "Oh, I hate this thing

KIS. Few women want to kiss a man with such a tangle of facial hair!" told her brother, looking into his eyes.

'KIS looked priceless, big and ugly right now,' Becky thought. He didn't know what to say, 'but then that's why God made older sisters,' she imagined.

"Where did you find this miracle?" Wela questioned him. "I thought you said you were just going fishing? It looks to me like you caught an angel."

KIS shrugged his shoulders, "She fell from the sky, right into a Mangrove pool. It was a miracle she didn't die."

Wela looked to her upper right, then turned back to face the young couple, "This is powerful medicine. Do you know that? It's synchronicity! The Spirits have spoken to you two. I always knew there was magic among the mangroves. It's divine intervention, KIS. You need to love, honor, and cherish this woman. She's a gift to you from the Great Spirit."

Something strange inside KIS blossomed; he felt a light where there had been darkness. He felt renewed. He answered solemnly, "I will."

Becky strangely gravitated to KIS's side. This giant of a man who had proven his worth time and time again to her. She felt strangely excited to stand beside him, as Wela looked at her too, "And Becky you need to love, honor, and cherish this man, for richer for poorer, in sickness and in health, he who has saved you," Wela advised.

There was a mixture of feelings that exploded within Becky. She realized that Wela was pairing, she and KIS, if only in an informal way, but then again, isn't that what some Native American's do when they wed?

A wedding in olden days could occur with a simple handshake or just the nod of the head. The marriage agreement between a man and a woman, simply meant 'to stay' with each other, then to seal the bond intimately with a kiss, and to spend a night together among the stars. A marriage ceremony could be that simple, but strangely Becky felt this was right.

KIS brought Becky back into the present when he looked at Wela, "Reminds me, being an elder of the village and Justice of the Peace, is my credit good at your general store? Becky could use some fresh clothes and especially shoes that fit?"

Becky was stunned and surprised, "Justice of the Peace?" she gasped.

Wela grinned and winked at her newfound friend, "Among my other duties in the tribe. I'd love to go to Law School, to be able to fight to protect the Everglades and our village, using the white man's own laws, but, I don't have the money. Education is very expensive and our tribe is poor."

Becky interrupted, softly asking, "Did you just marry us?"

Wela leaned down and kissed Becky tenderly on the cheek, "Girl, something very magical has happened between you and KIS, if you haven't had time to put it together. You fell from a moving airplane into those Mangroves. You've been given a second life! You could've been killed, but you were spared. Did you ever ask yourself why? You were given extra time on earth. Don't waste this spiritual gift with hesitancy."

Becky did know that she had spent all her life alone, hoping for Mr. Right to come into her life. She hadn't ever envisioned this Beast, her Monster from the Black Lagoon, but he was thawing. She felt she had influence over him. She felt something magical happening to her and the way he looked at her in return. She remembered her grandmother talking about the years during World War II, "Becky, not all women get the gift of a long courtship. Sometimes she needs to take her man, before he spins off out of her reach. Love is too precious to lose. When the time is right, you'll know. Your heart will sing to you. You'll want to spend your life with this man, your soul mate."

Looking impishly at both KIS and Becky, Wela told them, "You two are going out into the swamp, alone. Nature may show herself to you two. Should you both act on your feelings,

I've put my blessing on your union. We could fill out all the legal paperwork later. I can formally marry you when there's more time, IF you choose to spend your lives together. I'm just a cautious woman," she smiled softly, "I'm your older sister."

Becky hugged Wela as Wela turned her towards the village's general store, "Girl, we need to go spend some of KIS's money."

Becky didn't know much about KIS, this strange new man in her life, "Does he have money?" she asked.

Wela looked down, "He has some. He's been industrious this past year, even though he's mourned Osola's absence. Whether KIS knows it or not, Osola is here with us, in spirit. But," looking at Becky, Wela added, "I've a feeling KIS has a new friend now, a very female one, a woman who is just starting to feel all of her abilities?"

Becky slowly smiled. She was feeling sensations she hadn't ever felt before. Her heart was opening. She felt a new light was coming into her life.

KIS reached into the airboat and shouldered the duffle bag, following the women to the village general store. As he walked up the ramp to solid ground, he passed Pima.

"What's in the bag, KIS?" Pima sneered, "Afraid us stupid Injuns will steal your stuff?"

KIS knew that wasn't going to happen. He was inside his family's village. People were close here; stealing just 'wasn't done.

"No, Pima," I wouldn't insult the village that way, but these are Becky's things. I'm not sure what she'll want," KIS answered patiently.

"Now you're carrying a woman's belongings around, KIS? The Great Warrior sniffs after a woman's skirt?" he taunted.

KIS stiffened, but then asked in a measured tone, "Pima, why are you still angry with me?"

"Because you let my brother die. That my brother threw his life away on a white man!" Pima spat at KIS.

"Pima, I've thought about that over and over in my head for the last year, and I can't explain it, I can't change it. I was supposed to die over there not Owl. I've tempted death out in the swamp each day for a year now trying to join Owl, but it didn't work. I wish you'd find it in your heart to forgive me, Pima," KIS confessed. "It's not good for us have bad feelings between us."

"I'll hate you forever, KIS," Pima shouted angrily as he ran away.

Wela's soft words of a little while ago, caught KIS's attention, like the call of the bird. 'It was uncanny that Wela had for all intents and purposes married Becky and he, but yet, she still left the back door open to them both, should their feelings prove different. He couldn't deny feeling a master plan at work, some manifestation of fact. That both Becky and he had cheated death so many times, to come together. There has to be a higher force directing our paths,' he thought.

His footsteps carried him to the general store. Luckily, Sanchez the barber was still there.

"I need a shave and to get GI again, Sanchez. You know the routine," KIS placed his order.

Sanchez smiled, "Like old times eh, KIS? Like when Osola and you were preparing to go back into the white man's world? When you two were preparing for war?"

"I don't know about the war part, Sanchez," KIS answered honestly, "but there is a girl, I'd like to get closer to," he said, looking over at the women.

Becky was excitedly holding up, examining a pure white dress as their eyes met. She had a gleam in her eye, but a questioning look on her eyebrow, as she looked at him. His eyes warmly answered her questioning look. He knew she was a holy vision to him.

Becky got what she needed as far as a few outfits. More importantly, she got a pair of sneakers that actually fit her.

KIS didn't recognize the stranger looking back at him in

the barbershop mirror. He was GI again. It had been almost a year, since he last looked like this. He was starting to feel like his old self again.

Wela was wrapping Becky's new clothes, "OH, who's this tall, blond, and handsome man," Wela asked Becky, as KIS walked up to them at the counter.

"Oh my gosh, is that you KIS? I wouldn't have recognized you without the smelly beard and dirty-tangled dread-locks," she laughed.

Worriedly, KIS asked, "Do I look ok?" he asked questioningly.

Becky rubbed her hand over his clean-shaven face and looked directly into his bright blue eyes, "You look fine cowboy. You clean up, nice."

Chapter 10

KIS shouldered the duffle bag and the large bag of Becky's new clothes. Wela walked with the two back to the airboat, moored at the pier along the canal.

"Where are you going now?" Wela looked at first KIS and then Becky.

KIS threw the duffle in the boat, stepped in and then carefully put Becky's clothes where they wouldn't get wet. "I thought we'd go to the island," he said, "to give us a chance to think. It's been a whirlwind of events up to this point. We've mostly been reacting to threats so far. We need to plan out what we want to do, where we want to go," KIS explained, looking at Becky for her reaction.

Becky peered at her two new friends, little more than strangers really, but these people had helped her. "The island? Will I be safe there?"

Wela straightened critically, "The island is a nice term for a bit of peat and tangled roots of mangrove trees, more like a toilet KIS calls home these days."

"Oh, lovely," Becky rolled her eyes sarcastically.

KIS piped up defensively, looking at her, "Wela's being too stern I think. The island isn't bad, just rustic," he smiled, trying to ease her fears.

"Ah-huh," Becky laughed nervously, "There're dirt floors and outdoor plumbing I assume. My Father was a real estate genius. Real estate terms have hidden meanings for those in the business. Like: 'cozy' means a house the size of a closet ,or 'rustic' meaning a house you'd find way back in the hills."

"Touché," KIS waved his arm in a sweeping motion, as he then reached out to help her into their newly inherited airboat. "En guarde," he offered with a sly twinkle in his eyes, the duel begins,"

As Becky climbed to her elevated chair behind his, she passed his face and drew her finger along his arm, "I prefer to salsa, a dance of passion and romance, of dancing closely, touching each other gently, rather than a duel," she fluttered, her long dark eyelashes at her giant Nordic Prince.

"Ah," Wela laughed. "You two were made to be a couple I think, to help each other in life. I can feel the heat from you two. I sense a blending of spirits. I see a compliment of talents to reach common goals. All of this is a good omen."

Wela sobered, "KIS, I need to warn you both. Pima says there are men asking around, about a single woman wandering lost in the Glades."

KIS raised his eyebrows at the warning. Wela added, "Pima says this woman has mucho money of the drug lords and that there's a reward being offered for her return. Either way, all this talk of money is a temptation to the poor people who live in the Glades. Keep a watchful eye on the horizon and your ears alert for strange sounds. It might be more than spirits walking up behind you."

"Has Mo been by, asking about me?" KIS looked at Wela.

Becky remembered Mo was KIS's sheriff friend. He'd told her about Mo after he'd downed the helicopter.

Wela looked solemnly at KIS, "Mo said he was going fishing in the Keys for a few days, and that you're a big boy. He also said if they come after you, they'd better bring body bags, but also for you not to make too much noise."

KIS nodded as he sat in the front seat, "That's Mo's way of sayin if he doesn't know about something then he doesn't have to deal with it. He also said keep the action quiet, so not to attract attention. I'm on my own with these bad boys, but that's ok," he said to both women as he reached down to start the airboat's engine, to begin their journey home. He felt uneasy. 'Was he putting his friends and neighbors in a position of temptation?' he wondered. 'Were he and Becky safe in the Glades any more? Maybe they'd be ok for a bit, but where would they go from here? What to do next?' these thoughts haunted him.

The trip through the winding canals of the Glades from the Indian village to KIS's island took about an hour and a half. They kept heading north for an hour and then veered slightly northeast into the Devil's Garden. The drone of the engine and swoosh of the propeller made talking nearly impossible.

This gave Cathy a chance to talk to Becky in a silent, mental chat. 'What are you getting us into this time, Becky?" Cathy started the conversation. 'We don't even know this guy from Adam really.'

'Oh, hush up,' Becky silently answered. 'He's protected us against alligators, poisonous snakes, and drug hit men numerous times all in twenty-four hours. How much more do we need to know before we feel safe with him? Who should I feel safe with? I'm TIRED of running, tired of trying to find my Mr. Right. Maybe he's right here right in front of me. Maybe a divine power has brought us together in this nasty swamp?'

'He is a rugged beast, a real panther in the wilderness, I'll say that for him,' Cathy said huskily, ',but you're a tigress from the urban jungle. Will you two have anything in common? I mean after this fight is over?'

Becky thought for a moment, trying to think it through. 'I sense we have common ideas. We sure are different kinds of people, but isn't that what makes life interesting, the spice of life? I think we can compromise. He's a reasonable man and he hasn't hurt me in any way. He hasn't tried to dominate me, where it's his way or no way. What else could a woman ask for in a man?'

Cathy had to agree, but smiled an impish smile, 'I wonder if the saying about the size of his hands, is really true?'

Becky blushed, 'You shush up! You're just too terrible for words, Cathy.'

Finally, on the horizon, KIS pointed with his right arm at a break in the ocean of saw grass, a cluster of tangled trees and vines, evidenced by the green bushy appearance of the tree's leaves and limbs, lay ahead.

"Is that your home?" Becky shouted against the blast of wind.

KIS nodded, "The Glades mostly are a grass covered prairie under a thin covering of water most of the year," he shouted back, "veined with canals to navigate around, that hold some water during the dry season. This swamp has two seasons a year really, the wet in the summer and the dry in the winter." He turned his head, "Occasionally one will find a cluster of trees that have a soft floor of sand and peat. That's an island here in the Glades. High ground might only be six inches above the surrounding water."

Becky nodded, seeing that there was a canal circling KIS's island. There was a small indentation in the vegetation, what one might call a cove, on the westerly side of the island, only wide enough to tie up one or two boats. KIS headed the airboat towards the cove, riding well up onto the loamy ground. He jumped down to tie their airboat securely to a tree.

He stepped back into the boat to help Becky down from her perched seat, "Once on shore, you have to get used to the footing," he warned. "It's a little like walking on a waterbed," he tried to give her an analogy.

"Thanks for the warning," she said looking around. "From the way you jumped down and tied up to that tree, I'd say you've been here for a long time?"

KIS went strangely loose, relaxing; "Owl and I have used this island as a hunting camp for many years. After I got out of the Corp, I had nowhere else to go, so I came back here to be with Owl," sadly adding, "but he's not here. I've been all alone for the last year. It wasn't what I wanted. Just the way things turned out, I guess. I prayed for an answer, a direction in my life, and then you suddenly appeared, out of the sky, saying you have no one either, and nowhere to go. I thought, I thought maybe you were a sign. That you were the answer to my prayers," he confessed shyly.

His honesty gave her goose bumps. She leaned towards him and softly said, "Thanks for being so open with me about your thoughts. I appreciate you letting me know how you feel. That's important to me."

He looked into her face, extended his massive hand and gently touched her arm almost reverently. She felt a spark that went directly to her heart.

He then reached into the airboat to grab their bags. A large tree, an ancient laurel oak, looking similar to a large maple tree, dominated the interior of the island. Its lower branches had died leaving only the upper branches alive. They both caught the sunlight, but also made a natural living space under its upper branches.

"Where's your house?" Becky looked around.

KIS pointed, "Up there."

"In the tree?" Becky half laughed in surprise. "I thought boys and tree houses parted company when they passed the age of ten?" she grinned.

KIS wasn't offended by his tiny female guest, "Men can be boys inside," he confided a male secret. "I guess a good man is mostly responsible, but deep inside, he should have a touch of little boy in him, to make things interesting," he smiled. On a practical side he added, "It's handy the house is that way," he explained. "If the water level rises, we're off the floor of the island and will stay dry. Also, being elevated, predators that hunt at night, usually don't climb trees."

"Predators?" she cringed, "Two or four legged?" she wanted to know.

KIS laughed, like an inside joke, "Well, the island is

actually cut in half. George is on one side and Edward is on the other."

Becky looked confused, "I only have room in my life for one man, and I'm not into a foursome. I don't flirt," but admitted, "although I'm somewhat of a social butterfly. I do like parties, but parties of my choosing," she specified. She added, "I don't want my man flirting with other women."

KIS held up his hands gently defensive, "I'm glad you don't like to flirt with other guys, cause, I want my woman's attention on me. I don't want to be possessive, but I want to clearly know you're mine, or we need to part."

Becky came close to his chest, "When a man allows his woman some space, she appreciates that, and the freedom draws her closer to him than if he put chains around her," she breathed.

He smiled and noted her feminine lesson. He continued his tour of the island, "You shouldn't go over this way," he pointed to the north end of the island, "That's Edward's domain. Edward is a Burmese Python, who keeps the rodent population on the island down, be they rat or mouse, anything that scampers on the ground."

Becky gasped nonplused, "A PYTHON?"

He nodded, "Yep, pretty hard to believe in America, but these pythons' ancestors were once a pet that the owners didn't want anymore. The owners dumped the snakes in a canal somewhere awhile back. The swamp is ideal for the pythons to survive and grow in numbers. Years ago, the alligator was the King of the Glades, but now pythons are battling alligators for dominance here."

KIS went on with the island tour, giving her a look at his home, "And to the south side, is the outside latrine, which I'd only recommend using during daylight. If you need a long stay, I'd recommend taking care of that during the day. George, an ancient twenty foot-long alligator, doesn't lumber around then. He's out feeding somewhere in the Glades. Both

Edward and George are like dangerous pets. At night, he and Edward roam their domains and guard the island for me. We won't be surprised at night by intruders."

KIS walked over to a ring of stones used as a fire pit, and put together a fire, "Do you cook?" he asked her.

She looked sheepish, "That's one thing, I was going to talk to you about KIS. I'm not very domestic," she confessed, "I don't think I'd be a good housewife. I had servants do all the household chores when I was growing up."

KIS thought about this turn of events and shrugged, "I love to cook."

Becky's eyes brightened, 'maybe this could work?' she wondered.

KIS added, "When I don't feel like cooking, I'll take you out to dinner," he answered himself, pleased.

"I can do that," she grinned.

"Do you like fish?" he looked at her.

She shrugged, "Not really. I'm not much of a seafood person. I'm a meat and potatoes girl, born and bred in the Midwest, raised on beef or bacon."

"I'll have to work on that," he confided. "I only have perch in the refrigerator today. Is this ok for now?"

"Perch will work in a pinch. Do you mind if I use the ladies while you cook us dinner?" she asked shyly.

KIS lumbered off to the shoreline where he had some live perch swimming around on a string, "The door doesn't shut that well and has an open back", he yelled over his shoulder, not looking back. Grinning he said under his breath, "George likes to sneak up on people in the latrine sometimes."

"He did say the gator was out hunting during the day right?" Cathy questioned. "'Literally, you're betting your bum when you sit on his throne if you're wrong,' she thought.

KIS cleaned the fish at the shoreline; he then rubbed them down with some special spices, he kept in a glass jar. Then he put two fish on sticks over the fire. Finally, they had a peaceful moment to relax.

"KIS, I was wondering," she began.

He looked up at first, but then quietly went back tending the fire, "Yup?"

"I've told you I'm not domestic, and you said that was ok with you?"

"Yup, I don't mind as long as you keep yourself clean and neat," he answered, "but if we're together, I want to know you're mine with no doubt between us."

'Works for me,' she thought, but added, "If we're to live together, what would you think if I had a hobby?"

"Like sewing or pottery?" he wondered, "something girly like that?"

She swerved, "Well, not exactly," she tried to put this delicately. "I'm not much of a wall flower type girl," she confessed honestly. "I wanted to put a computer in an office I'd have in the house, or anywhere we are really. My mom was a whiz at the stock market, and she taught me a lot. To me, the stock market is like a game, and I'm great with numbers. I'd like to take some money and play with it, see where I can go," she confessed. "The stock market is a wonderful place, if done right, where people with new ideas can get money to make their ideas come to life." Then her mood darkened, "I hate corporations who withhold new advances, like cures for diseases that could save people's lives, just so they can protect worthless treatments to make more money or profit."

"KIS looked at her seriously, "There are things you haven't told me, like, I thought you were an orphan?"

Becky said flatly, "I didn't say that. I said I had no one, which to me is true. I have a mother and father, but I don't recognize them as having any part in my life now." She explained, "I was raised by a domineering corporate mother who only bore me, since I was A MISTAKE to her, and she hated me for being alive. I ran away from home in Chicago, because 'mother' wanted me to duplicate her sterile life, but I'd rather die first. If you're not sure about me, feel free to ask. I want to be honest with you too."

KIS knew how she felt. He felt the same when he ran away from his Uncle's farm to join the Marines. He couldn't find fault with her for that. Everyone has skeletons hiding in their past, but he knew people are who they choose to be, either good or bad. Humans have freedom of choice.

"Are you over eighteen?" he looked worried. "I don't want to go to jail for dating a minor."

Becky smiled, "No, you won't go to jail, I'm eighteen. I'm legal."

KIS took a fish off of the stick, put it on a plate and handed it to her, "Hope you like it. I favor a dry rub on fish or game."

"WOW," she exclaimed, "this is great! It must be the spices. I'm really a barbeque slut," she told him giggling. "Barbeque is a passion of mine."

She looked at KIS, "What about you? Do you have a passion too? What kinds of food do you like?

He took a bite of his perch, "I like See-Food," he answered first. "I see it and then I eat it," he grinned. "Being ex-military I'm used to all kinds of food, especially being made to eat something, I didn't choose myself. Maybe you can help teach me how to relax, to enjoy the finer points of life? I haven't had much peace. I don't know how to be gentle, but I'm learning with you. I'm afraid to touch you. I'm afraid I'll break you, you're so tiny."

'Oh gosh, he has a sense of humor,' Cathy chimed in.

Becky smiled, "I can help you learn about life and the finer things of being pleasing to a lady. Like are you a good kisser? That's important to a woman," she told him.

KIS blinked, "I don't know. I haven't had many chances to practice."

"That's a NO," Becky answered herself, looked upward.

Becky, smiled, whirling her hand around, "and?"

He stopped eating for a minute, "Well, you know I love machines. I'm a pilot, but love planes and boats. I'm a little quirky," he hesitated.

'What's this?' Cathy yelled, thinking she found a dent in his armor.

"In what way?" Becky urged.

KIS turned red and answered, "I like gold."

Her eyes widened, "I don't understand the problem? Everyone likes gold, unless, you go crazy over it," she looked at him cautiously, thinking, 'I'm a bling girl myself.'

Like she had opened a can of worms, KIS started, "I am a modern day prospector. It isn't like I have gold fever or anything serious like that, but I love the idea of finding gold. Be it prospecting, mining, or treasure hunting."

'Sounds interesting,' she thought. 'Something we can do in our free time'. "Ok, and?" Becky answered, digging for more.

This was evidently a favorite subject with KIS, "A lot of gold mines stopped producing gold back in the day, because the cost of digging cost more than the selling price. Of course these days there aren't big chunks lying around usually, but even small nuggets or powder is worth a good bit in today's market. It's something I'd like to pursue, if I ever had the chance. It's a lot like you and your stock market, I guess," KIS offered, "It's a game to me."

It was getting late and the sun was starting to set. Becky was getting tired, but she wondered, 'Cathy, can you bunk out tonight?'

'You mean? Really? You're gonna?' Cathy blurted.

Cathy didn't get an answer, as Becky stood up and sat next to KIS, leaning into him as their lips met slowly, tenderly, in a kiss that would have ignited a rock.

As KIS picked Becky up and carried her off to their tree house, Cathy called out, 'I want DETAILS!'

Chapter 11

"Hey, Cowtown," Aggie complained, leaning against the crumbling mud wall in the abandoned roofless farmhouse, "I'm so freekin cold my nipples'll cut glass. Can't you throw one of them cow chips on the fire and get us some heat agoin? I can't get warm!" Aggie wore all the clothes he had and was tryin his best to cocoon himself in his poncho.

Cowtown looked at his cousin, "There ain't no cows in this God forsaken frozen desert, Aggie." He held a road pie, "This here is gen-u-ine camel poo."

Aggie blinked, "Oh, Wow. I never thought I'd be this desperate to get warm. My recruiter never said nothing about freezing to death while smellin camel poo, or I know he never said we'd be 20 miles behind enemy lines with 320,000 Iraqi Imperial Guard Troops just itchin to slit our throats." He looked accusingly at Cowtown; "I let you talk me into join up an fight for freedom?"

Cowtown looked offended, "There you go again, Aggie. You ain't gonna let it go that I got you to join up with me on the buddy system and be a Marine. OK, I'm a really bad guy for wanting to do more than work in my Dad's feed store for the rest of my life. I guess it's a sin to want to see more of the world?" He confessed, "My dad and mom married right out of high school, they had me right off, and never left Fort Worth. Heck, they think its something special to go over to Dallas every year to the State Fair." He looked angrily at Aggie, "I guess I made you join? You, being the rocket scientist you are an all?"

Aggie felt bad, "Naw, couz. Being honest, I was only going to marry Suzie Johnson, work in the stock yards, and raise a bunch of kids." He huddled back in his poncho, "I wanted to see more of the world too. If I hadn't been bangin Suzie so much and playin football in high school, I should've studied and gone ta college. I wish Suzie were in my arms now. I should've told her I loved her more than I did. I'd give anything to smell her hair now. Hope she'll wait for me?" He held up her letters, "At least she still writes to me. I have hope."

Angie was Lance Corporal Rick Anderson hailing from Austin and his cousin Cowtown or Lance Corporal Jakob Evers of Fort Worth were the rear guard for the 5th Sniper Squad, 1st Special Warfare Platoon. Snowy or Corporal John Walters from a small rural town in Colorado and Guard Leader for the Squad, on watch now, piped up, "Don't be making that fire too big guys. We're twenty miles deep in Injin Country, an all alone. There's nothing as far as the eye can see, but after dark, put that fire out. We'll just have to freeze through the night. Way out here in the desert, light travels far. I don't want to get ambushed."

Snowy tucked in his head into his fatigue jacket that was stiff with frost. Fifth Squad had been on this behind the lines' mission for the last three weeks and the temperature hadn't gotten above twenty-five degrees the whole time. "Why can't the Corp ever have a war where it's nice, a place worth bleedin or dyin for?" he groused.

Aggie looked at Owl, who was Corporal Osola Lightning, a full-blooded Indian from Florida and Sarge's spotter, "Where's Sarge, Owl? Where's the Ice Princess?" Aggie asked dripping with sarcasm.

Owl shot Aggie a piercing stare, "Why'd you call KIS that? He's not cold at all. You just don't know him," Owl looked angry, "you haven't taken the time to know him."

Aggie didn't let it go as he opened his MRE, meal ready to eat, "And you do Owl? You know the Sarge? So tell us how a grown man lets himself be called KIS? Sounds like some fag pop group with face paint from back in the seventies."

Cowtown sat down, opened his Cajun rice with beef sausage MRE, Aggie took out a Beef enchilada. Snowy still kept watch but stopped to listen.

Owl took out chicken pesto pasta MRE and started, "Yeah, KIS, and I go way back, eight years now. We were boots together back on the island."

All the squad members knew what being friends back on The Island meant. Paris Island, where boys become men. The process changes a man forever. A friend who went through that with you is very special, very close.

Owl took a bite of his food and talked, "KIS was in my Platoon in Boot Camp. He was an orphan from Sunbury, Pennsylvania, I think. He knew his parents before they died in a car crash. That was tough on him. Seein people killed at that early age. He was sent to his uncle's farm in Lancaster after his folks died. His uncle was pretty religious and they didn't get along. So when KIS was sixteen, he ran away and joined up. With KIS being the giant, six feet three, and two hundred forty pounds of solid muscle, except for his white-blond hair, he looked like a draft horse." Owl looked puzzled, "First time my older sister, Wela, saw KIS, she said he looked like a medieval, northern-Saxon knight, whatever that means. Girls! Who knows how they think?" he shrugged. "When the recruiter saw KIS for the first time, all he saw as a guy big enough to carry a Squad M-60 light machinegun without complaint and all the ammo that goes with that. That's gotta add sixty pounds to a grunts pack, at least."

Aggie, Cowtown and even Snowy sat speechless after hearing KIS's story. Their Sergeant was a real loner, intimidating from his size, but it was his inner lethality that scared them the most. Like the guy could cut your head off, be covered in your blood head to toe, and not blink an eye. He was that stone cold. 'Death on Wheels,' they called him.

Owl took out his canteen, took a swig then, "KIS, and I met on the rifle range. We both were great shots, the best of our platoon. The DIs paired us together; we traded off being shooter and spotter. We went through AIT and then sniper school together. The Head Instructor at sniper school made KIS the shooter, because he said KIS was a born killer. He explained only one man in two million have a personality like walking death. KIS has that gift or curse."

"Owl, why do they call the Sarge, KIS?" Cowtown asked.

Owl grinned a sly grin, "You want the official version?"

"First," Aggie gave a belly laugh, "then tell us 'the other' story." Aggie knew all military men have nicknames, usually not chosen by the owner. The nickname describes something about the person, or just to chafe his butt.

Owl sat up straight, out of respect, "KIS is Sergeant Kyle Ibsen Swoboda. All snipers have call signs that are assigned at sniper school. The Lead Instructor used the Sarge's initials KIS for his call sign, KIS of Death. One shot, one kill."

Owl finished his chow; "You guys got KIS all wrong."

"How so, Owl?" Snowy challenged back.

"You guys came into the Fifth Squad after the Panama Operation," Owl pointed out, "you are the replacements for three of our men who died there. That operation was a real mess. We were to parachute behind enemy lines like we always do and create confusion before the major invasion, but we got dropped in the wrong place. Some of our equipment failed, and three of our men got killed mighty quick. It was a shock! KIS helped start the Fifth Squad. He personally recruited those men we buried. When they died, it was like someone cut out part of his heart, what little is left. It was like his parents, dying on him, leavin him alone again. I worked real hard to bring him out of his shell. That Operation erased all my hard work. Woosh, down the toilet! KIS became more of a loner after that. It was like he was afraid to let himself get to know a person, fearful they would only die on him."

Everyone in the quiet circle blinked. That story had stunned them all.

Owl got quiet, "This is just between us, right?"

Aggie, Cowtown, and Snowy all nodded. This was a secret they knew.

"KIS never had a girlfriend. He's not been with a woman," Owl confided.

All three dudes cringed. Aggie broke the thick silence.

"You mean the Sarge is still cherry?" he half-squeaked half-laughed.

Both Snowy and Owl started for Aggie. They were gonna kill him, but Aggie shot up his hands in surrender, "Alright. I shouldn't have said that," Aggie groused, but smiled asking, "What's the matter? He too small he can't get a girl?"

Cowtown punched Aggie in the shoulder, "You know couz, you can be a real creep sometimes? I oughta throw you in the fire, for comments like that."

Aggie started to feel bad, but good. He had dissed KIS quite a bit.

Owl got serious, "Guys, KIS and I are finishing our second hitch, eight long years in the Corp. When we got back from our last leave, KIS, and I were trying to turn in our discharge papers and get out. I wanted to start a gator farm in Florida and KIS almost has his bachelor's degree in mechanical engineering. He's already a commercial pilot. KIS can write his ticket anywhere, but he wanted to start a charter company in my hometown to fly fishermen around in an amphibious plane or use an airboat to get them to hard to reach to spots."

"Wow," Cowtown exhaled. "Did you get your discharge papers in?"

"Yes and no," Owl shrugged. "The First Sergeant took our papers, but we were frozen in place, then shipped over here."

Aggie thought, 'You never know what another man is going through,' but then he brightened, "Owl, you said there was the un-official version of KIS?"

Owl smiled, "Yep and it's awesome! We had just finished AIT and were waiting for a bus to take us to Sniper School.

We were sitting in a little rib shack just outside Lejeune; you know those cheap dives run by a mom and pop? The kind of place where they have a hickory smoker outside churnin out baby back ribs caramelized in sweet-hot barbeque sauce that's lick your fingers good? "

Aggie, Cowtown, and Snowy grinned. They knew what Owl was talking about. There was butcher paper for table clothes, and you had to watch you didn't get caught in fly tape when you walked around inside the restaurant.

"Well, like I said," Owl went on, "we were sitting at the counter, all of us havin a brewsky, but KIS. KIS doesn't drink. Momma Shirley comes out front from the kitchen paddlin around in her size thirteen combat boots, looking like a huge female mud wrestler, goin 380 pound at least. She sees KIS, the biggest Marine of our bunch, suckin on an orange soda. Momma looks at KIS and asks, "And who's this lumberjack? Honey, you look like a man my size! What's your name Sugaplum? I need to get to know you better! You a REAL man."

Owl starts to laugh so hard he almost wet himself. "KIS answered Momma flatly with 'Kyle'. One joker in our group was three sheets to the wind says, 'Momma Shirley, that's Kyle Ibsen Swoboda. He's not spoken for or nothing!' Now Momma got all the way through the 4th grade, but she had a good heart. Momma says, "OH, his initials are KIS," she sighed, her one front tooth showin, "Give us a kissy, KIS," she grinned and spat a stream of tobacco juice from the wad of broad-leaf in her right cheek, while batting her long eyelashes at him."

When everyone's toes uncurled and the laughter died, Owl got up. KIS had been gone a long time. The others tried to keep warm and get whatever sleep they could. It was going to be a long walk tonight. They had their job to do.

Far out in the frozen wasteland in the Kuwait desert, some distance from the bombed out farmhouse, a Marine sniper in desert camouflage uniform, crouched on the crest of a sand dune watching the sun perched on the distant horizon. The giant of a man was layered in all the clothes he had in a futile gesture against the icy desert wind. KIS felt somehow the sun was akin to his life. If one didn't know the time, the sun could've been rising or setting.

KIS stiffened for a heartbeat then relaxed as the sound of boots on desert sand approached. To anyone else, the sound would've been undetectable. Owl and he were now so close mentally they could nearly communicate through thoughts, without speaking. Speaking could be lethal to a sniper. Stealth and silence were their way of life. Owl stopped and crouched down on KIS's left side as KIS clutched his customized M-14 with silencer, muzzle pointing to the right as KIS was left handed.

"Time to go, KIS. Time to do your thang," Owl whispered.

KIS didn't look up, but kept staring at the distant sun on the horizon as he reached into his jacket pocket, pulled out two Ashten corona cigars, handing one to Owl. "I've got a strange feeling Owl. Like I'm going to die on this mission," KIS confided. He wasn't joking. He was cold serious. He nipped off the end of his cigar, spit it out, and lit it carefully, enjoying the smooth rich smoke, as he handed Owl the lighter.

Owl felt odd as he lit his cigar. "KIS, all combat soldiers get that feeling sooner or later. It's nothing new!" Owl exhaled. "You don't want to give into that feeling though, to make it happen. You're getting reckless Bro, like when you stormed into that house to save the downed pilot last week. You should've let the other guys go in first. You didn't even see the bad guy come up behind you with that eight-inch stiletto until he tried to pig-stick you. Lucky the blade bounced off a rib, and you turned in the other direction or you'd be a goner for sure. We'd be sendin you home in a body bag."

KIS harrumphed with resignation, "I got nothing to go home to Owl. You got Wela, yeah she's your older married sister, but she's at least female! Maybe she'll introduce you to some nice girl she knows. Girls are always trying to match people up, they do that kind-of-stuff, and you got your family too. I know we want to get out of the Corp. We were just one week too late to turn in our discharge papers before being sent over here to the War. Yeah, we want to start our own business just like every other grunt, you with your gator farm, but I don't have anything solid," he frowned, "I got no-one to go home to."

Owl clenched his cigar in his teeth as he moved to KIS's right side to move the layers of clothing away and check KIS's wound. Frozen blood marked the spot. "Dang KIS, you tore my nice stitches! Only thing keeping you from bleeding to death is that as fast as you bleed, it freezes."

Owl moved the clothing back as he thought with concern, "You going over the edge on me, Bro? You gettin the five-mile-stare?"

KIS puffed on his stogie and cracked a little smile, "Na Owl, I'm ok."

Owl was amazed. KIS's wound must hurt something fierce.

KIS changed the subject, "It was great to rescue that A-10 pilot. I felt good about that, like, we were doin something important, instead of just working at the grocery store back home. Livin the safe life. In the Corp, we do jobs NO-One else wants, but dirty jobs that have to be done. That's what makes us Special."

Owl smiled, "Yeah, the pilot called himself Montana."

KIS shrugged and smirked as he sucked on his expensive hand-rolled cigar, but Owl did notice the familiar twinkle in KIS's eye when he's havin fun.

Owl had to laugh to himself. He hadn't seen KIS smile in a long time.

Owl, shaking his head in resignation said, "Come back to camp KIS before nightfall, so I can stitch you up again. That cross-stitch course we ordered from the TV really helped my sewing. I have to boil some water to unfreeze that blood first, and I don't want to light the stove after dark."

KIS silently nodded as Owl got up and walked back to the bombed-out farmhouse two hundred yards away. KIS finished smoking his cigar, which was rare. Usually he and Owl only chewed tobacco a vice, they picked up in Boot Camp from some of the southern boys. In the field, on a mission, tobacco smoke can give away your position and can be your death.

Owl walked up to Snowy who was on guard. It was starting to grow dark.

A strange illumination in Snowy's hand caught Owl's attention, "What cha got there Snowy?" Owl asked curiously.

Snowy intently peered out into the darkness of the frozen desert as he rubbed a pennant, "Its my lucky charm, Owl. It was a gift to me when I was a boy. It's brought me luck ever since."

Snowy held out the necklace for Owl to see, but wouldn't let Owl hold it. That was another thing that caught Owl's attention. Snowy was a very warm and sharing fella, but this pennant he kept close to him, at all times.

Owl looked at the blue iridescent medallion, "Wow, that looks like Aztec markings in the metal. It looks Native American to me."

Snowy kept rubbing the necklace; "I got it from a white man who was paler than most folks around I'd seen, a stranger, one day when I was a young boy. I was up in the mountains near our ranch in Colorado in late fall, just before the first snow. My dog ran ahead and I thought I'd lost him, but in a little while, I found Rusty sitting next to this stranger sitting on a deadfall. The stranger was petting him like, he was used to animals. When I came up on them, the man asked if Rusty was my dog, and I said yes. He said he hadn't seen his pet for a long time, and he missed him terribly. Rusty's spirit reminded him of his pet back home, and that I must be someone special for Rusty to stay with me. We talked for a while. When it was time to leave, the stranger thanked me for sharing my dog with him for a little while, and asked me not to say that we'd met to anyone. I agreed and the guy gave me this necklace in thanks. He said it would bring me good luck and not to take it off."

"Wow, that sounds mystical," Owl, commented, "If you were Indian, I'd say you had been visited by the Great Spirit or one of his Lower Chiefs."

"I'm not Indian, but I agree with you. I'd never seen that guy before and our family knew everyone for fifty miles around. Our hometown only has nine year-round residents. Lord, everyone knows everyone and we're all cousins."

Owl knew what Snowy was talking about. His village only had 35 people living in it. Small town people know everything about each other.

Aggie looked over at Owl, "How's the Sarge Owl?"

Owl glanced at Aggie pleased with the softening in his tone, "He's fine. He's taking a break. He'll be here shortly."

Snowy snapped his fingers together once, three heads snapped around. KIS silently appeared out of nowhere and moved into the ruined farmhouse like a silent wind. He headed over to Owl and sat down.

Owl didn't want to waste time. The sunlight would soon die and with a new moon, the night would be pitch-black, perfect to march the twelve miles to their prairie dog mound, that was their next shooting position. Last night they were resupplied with just food and another 1000 rounds of ammo. This was their third resupply drop. The 5th Squad had been busy dispensing death, disrupting the ruthlessly confident enemy.

Owl looked at Aggie and Cowtown, "Rig your two man tent together over us as I tend KIS's wound to shield the light."

The two men covered KIS and Owl silently as they were told. They didn't need to be told twice.

KIS took the MRE that Owl handed him. Owl had saved his favorite, chicken and rice. Owl soaked and thawed layers of clothing that were stiff with frozen blood until he could see the wound.

"Dang, KIS, you ripped out my stitches. You move too fast with a wound like this," Owl complained.

"You worry too much, Owl," KIS sighed.

"KIS, you belong in a hospital. Maybe Snowy should call in and cancel the mission?"

KIS frowned, "If we do buddy, a lot of our guys are gonna die when they run into those thirty tanks and all their support troops. It'll be a slaughter."

Owl knew the facts of the Iraqi invasion of Kuwait in August. Iraq had the military might that seriously rivaled the United States. They had almost the same number of modern tanks and worst of all their national leaders didn't hesitate to use their weapon to kill people. This was evident in their long war with Iran where Iraq used unconventional, like gas warfare, to kill their enemies.

Then in August 1991, Iraq figured they would be unopposed by the world when they invaded the small oil-rich, peaceful tiny nation of Kuwait, saying that Iraq was annexing the small country. Now Iraq controlled almost twenty percent of the world's oil production.

Worse yet, Iraq secretly was developing a nuclear weapon capability. The heart-stopping fear was that they were almost ready to put the nuclear weapon on one of their missiles and fire the missile at Israel. This was the unthinkable to contaminate the major oil producing area of the world. Iraq felt comfortable in this aggression knowing that the Americans would be horrified if their loved ones in the military would be killed in long bloody battles over foreign oil. The Viet Nam war was still too fresh in the minds of the American people.

Owl silently nodded his head as he started to sew KIS's wound back together, "Should I use anesthetic? This is gonna hurt."

"You know I can't Owl. I need to be sharp tonight. We're all at the end of our endurance. Living outside in this freezing weather is sapping our strength. I don't want to make a mistake," KIS grimaced.

Owl understood this but complained, "Wela made me promise to get you home alive. You aren't making my job easy you know."

KIS didn't answer as he allowed his mind to wonder, to think of his home in Sunbury, Pennsylvania. He was a coal-cracker, a person from the coal-mining region. He loved the dry cold snowy mountains in winter and the cool fishing streams in summer. That's why he liked being with Owl and his family. At least they lived near water.

Owl folded KIS's clothing back after bandaging the long ragged gash on KIS's right flank. None of the men had a second set of clothes to change into. Their mission wasn't a cakewalk. It was hard dirty work but somebody had to be crazy enough to do it. They traveled light, with only ammunition and food.

Owl emerged from the tent. Aggie and Cowtown, when Owl silently nodded, folded and stowed their tent halves. KIS motioned for Snowy to come close as KIS took out the familiar round tin of chewing tobacco and offered it to the four men. Snowy and Owl took healthy pinches and relished the practice of seating their poke between their lower lip and gum.

Aggie looked at Cowtown, "No way Bro. No wonder these guys are all single. No self-respecting girl would kiss any of them chewing that stuff."

The mention of girls got Cowtown talking about last summer at Billy-Rae's in the Fort Worth stockyards, "Aggie, remember when Suzie brought Amy, her girl friend up to meet me? Both girls wore those hoochie tops and short shorts last summer? Oh WOW, they both were stacked!"

Aggie laughed, "Ah yeah. Suzie brought her number one girlfriend for you. She hoped Amy and you'd take up together." Aggie couldn't help remembering, "You and Amy were really something! Boy - Couz, you and she were kissin so hot I thought you two would start a fire." Cowtown puffed up proud as a rooster. It was a warm day to remember.

Snowy spat a long stream of brown tobacco juice at a scorpion hole to cut off further talk about girls. He had to keep his men's mind on their guard jobs.

Aggie first looked at Snowy with his two-week beard stained brown with tobacco juice and then back to Cowtown, rolling his eyes, "I rest my case."

KIS took out his headset with boom microphone and put it on. Four other men did, likewise. It was time to go to work. Everyone put on his game face.

"Two," "Three," "Four," "Five," and "One" crackled in each man's earpieces. Owl was two, Snowy was three, Aggie was four, Cowtown was five, and KIS was one. Everyone was online.

"Ok guys, this is the night before the big game where we want to get into the playoffs, but our season can go either way," KIS talked to them all.

Cowtown looked at Aggie. Snowy looked at Owl.

"This is the end of our mission men. We do this and we can go home," KIS was being honest with his Squad. "This is where we need to earn our pay," he went on. "We're in the David and Goliath part of our mission. We're all frozen stiff and fightin to stay awake. We're where no one expects us to be, goin up against a very lethal enemy who wouldn't think twice of snuffing us. We have the element of surprise. This is what we do all the time, what we signed on for. We're all alone out here. If we trust in our training and each other, we can make a really big difference. If we make a mistake, we get a trip home in a flag draped box. Personally, I'm madder than a hornet. I plan on killing as many of those mothers, I can, before they spray our boys' guts all over this stinkin desert."

Well, there she was. KIS had laid the situation as it stood to his men.

"Three this is one. Take lead. Four and five bring up the rear. We're walking through at least one known mine field so everyone walks in the other guy's footprints or there won't be enough of you to send home in a shoe box."

Two, three, four, five, acknowledged over their scrambled signal, cloaked radios. KIS was the only member of the Fifth Squad, who had a radio that could talk to TAC-AIR and his team both at the same time. TAC-AIR was Air Force or Navy aircraft that they might work with when they were on a combat mission.

"Three-one, lead off." KIS was answered with, "three."

As Snowy led the squad off and the other four men followed, KIS took one last look around their camp to make sure their presence couldn't be detected. A blue iridescence on the white desert sand caught KIS's eye, and he picked it up. It was Snowy's necklace. "When I get a free minute, I'll give it back to Snowy,' KIS thought, putting the necklace in his fatigue jacket pocket.

Ten hours later, in a dying wind, the Fifth Squad approaching exhaustion in the below freezing desert, walked up a gully that led to a small hill of sand looking like a prairie dog mound in the middle of the desert. The night was pitch-dark. If it weren't for their night vision goggles, it would've been near impossible to walk. They were now about eight miles inside the Kuwait border, behind the defending Iraqi soldiers who were waiting to attack any Coalition troops trying to liberate Kuwait. Thirty Iraqi tanks were hidden six hundred yards to the south of the prairie dog mound. The squad had come from the north so their approach would be hidden from view by the mound of desert sand, which was their firing position.

Each man took a point on the compass and scanned their back trail for any enemy soldiers following them. A slow half hour passed then one squelch on the transmit button brought four thumbs-up. "Stand-down" cracked in their headsets. Three set the watch. We're gonna cover and sleep through the day and be ready for TAC-AIR to contact us at 2300 hr tomorrow night. Copy? Four silent thumbs up were shown. KIS added his own thumbs-up and Snowy covered his microphone and had a huddle with Aggie and Cowtown off the radio.

The day passed and the sun set again. At 2230 hours KIS's headset came alive, "KIS OF DEATH – Yanky Papa Leader, you up this freq?"

"Yanky Papa Lead – Rog – you got the KIS. Who's with ya?"

"KIS – YP Lead, we are a gaggle of three Alpha-10s loaded for bear, come back."

"Rog – YP Lead," KIS answered. "You're a little early. I hadn't expected you until 2300."

"KIS, this is Montana! When I saw this mission come up on the board, I though it'd be you and the boys. I didn't think anyone else would be ballzy enough for taking on all those tanks and 300 support troops single-handed. I wanted to come out and say thanks for the rescue in person. How are you and the squad?"

KIS smiled at Montana's voice, "We are really tired YP Lead. Let's get this party started. We're frozen stiff, want to get the job done, and go home!"

"Which direction do you want us to attack, KIS?" Montana shot back.

Cowtown twitched, catching KIS's attention. Cowtown held up a silent fist and three other bodies snapped rigid as boards. The attention was electrifying. KIS crawled over to Cowtown, who pointed two hundred yards out in the desert. A large combat patrol, of about thirty enemy soldiers, was following something. Oh my God, it was their trail into the prairie dog mound!

KIS's earpiece crackled, "KIS, are you OK?"

"YP Lead, hold high and dry. Back in a few, out," was all KIS whispered.

KIS partially heard as he watched the lead tracker in the enemy patrol suddenly stop about one hundred fifty yards from the squad's position, "Yanky Papa flight - Lead, orbit right on me now."

It was plain to see that the tracker had been following the Fifth Squad, but luckily the fickle desert wind had blown away their trail. There was a short enemy conference. It must've been decided that whoever had made the trail, no doubt, were Iraqi soldiers as the boot tracks were now unreadable. They thought NO coalition soldiers would be insane enough to come this close to their camp. At this point the enemy patrol continued south to the tank park, walking about fifty yards from KIS's position. When the enemy patrol was about two hundred yards to the south of the prairie dog mound, KIS contacted the TAC-AIR again.

"KIS – Lead, what happened?

"Lead – an enemy patrol just passed our position heading home. They must've been trailing us here."

"You ok? We need to party soon or we'll need to leave to refuel. We're approaching bingo gas."

In wars, there's always the unexpected. The unexpected can burn you.

As the enemy patrol passed KIS's position, everyone in the squad was so focused on the large patrol that they had missed the straggler. Every army has a sad sack, the screw up soldier. The Iraqi army wasn't any different.

The crack soldier's of the Fifth Sniper Squad missed Abdul, the screw up soldier who had lagged behind to take a dump. He was separated from the combat patrol, but wasn't in a rush to catch up. His sergeant was always yelling at him how bad a soldier he was. He saw this gully that he'd always wanted to explore, but wasn't ever allowed to. When he saw the mound of sand Abdul thought he could get some sleep and if lucky he'd miss KP in the morning.

As Abdul walked onto the top of the hill, what he saw definitely wasn't friendly. He saw three prone soldiers NOT holding familiar AK-47s to the left side and two soldier's looking at the tank camp through a telescopic sight. Snipers!

Abdul reacted to training and the sound of an AK-47 coming off safe caught people's attention. The three dark figures on the left swung at him with their rifles as one in a very threateningly way!

Green tracers from Abdul's AK laced the three soldiers laying down on the left, and then he swung his weapon to the right and cut loose a burst of more green tracers into the figure who jumped up to shield the man laying flat looking through the sniper rifle.

The man who shielded the sniper was lifted up and thrown back over the sniper, but suddenly a burst of white fireworks exploded in Abdul's head and then there was peace. KIS had pulled his silenced pistol and shot Abdul dead. KIS didn't realize in the confusion, he had bumped against the radio switch to both. Yanky Papa heard it all. All flight conversations are recorded. Everyone heard it.

KIS was on Owl fast, but he heard the unmistakable sound of a sucking chest wound and the sweet smell of blood. Owl knew he was going and only could manage, "KIS them for me Kyle. Goodbye to Wela – care - her."

KIS lost it, "Owl. Owl! Don't you dare die on me! You can't die. I'm the one to go, NOT YOU," KIS pleaded. Owl couldn't breathe with half his chest gone and just went limp. KIS was shocked to the core. It happened so quickly. It wasn't supposed to be like this!

YP Lead was immediately on the radio, "KIS! KIS? Are you OK?"

Dead air filled the radio. There was just static.

"KIS of Death – Yanky Papa Leader. Can you Charlie Mike?" Montana strained to hear his friends. "KIS, can you Continue the Mission?" It is tough to explain how close one becomes to fellow soldiers in war.

After a little while the radio crackled, "Montana they're gone! Its just me," KIS managed in plain English. He didn't think about radio protocol. It was very clear that KIS was totally shaken.

KIS half answered half thinking aloud, in plain English, over the radio, "Montana, my men are ALL DEAD! What've I DONE?" choking back these unfamiliar, overwhelming emotions. There's blood and gore everywhere.

Montana suddenly saw his targeting screen come alive with laser beams, indicating targets, tanks! Tracing the beams of light back pinpointed KIS's position. He couldn't believe his eyes. That crazy coal cracker was committing suicide! Unimaginable numbers of enemy soldiers were rushing KIS's position to turn off the laser beams.

"YP Lead, this is KIS of Death." Montana already started hearing KIS popping off 7.62 mm rounds from his M-14 as he faced his certain death like a man.

"KIS-YP Lead," Montana answered, choking back emotions and his tears as he answered the man who almost gave his life to save him, after being captured and tortured not a week ago. KIS was the man, HE owed his life to.

"Montana, the lights are on, the targets are hot. I started the music now Let's Dance!" KIS radioed through the sound of firing endless twenty-round magazines that seemed to go on for hours. The acrid smell of gunpowder and death soon filled the air.

KIS felt himself shaken as Becky worriedly cried, "KIS. KIS! Are you ok?"

KIS's eyes snapped open. For a minute, he wasn't sure where he was.

"I'm really sorry, Becky," KIS stammered, "I shouldn't have gone to sleep! This happens every time I sleep," he whispered.

"It seemed like you were having a nightmare?" Becky questioned him.

He slowly got control of himself, "All I know is, I can't sleep, or I relive my last two days of combat. The mission where I got all my men killed, and they pin a medal on me. They said I was brave, that I was a hero, but all I was doin was trying to kill as many of the enemy as I could, before they killed me. The docs call it PTSD, post traumatic stress disorder," KIS, covered in sweat, explained to Becky.

"Don't you ever sleep?" she asked, touching his heaving chest.

"Not if I can help it," he sighed. I know I got my men killed. They say I didn't do anything wrong, that I'm not at fault, but four of MY MEN are buried, and I'm still left alive. If I sleep, I relive the mission. So I just sit up each night and try to not sleep more than fifteen minutes at a time, or this happens." He looked at her, "You helped me relax when we were together tonight. You are amazing, an angel. You are the tenderness in my life, I never knew. The softness I never felt before," he told her moving his head shyly, confessing his heart to her.

Becky didn't know what to do, but she loved this monster more and more each day they were together. She was frightened beyond words, but women throughout history have dealt with their warrior husbands returning from battle. Somehow she would help KIS get over his nightmare; someway they would work out this problem of theirs. She was exhausted from the events of the last few days herself. She too had relaxed tonight as he held her in his massive arms. His joining with her soul had made her feel complete. She had fallen asleep peacefully. As she laid her head now on his massive chest, the smell of his masculine body, and the slowing of his heartbeat lulled her back to sleep.

Chapter 12

Soft light grew in the bedroom of the tree house as Becky opened her eyes. KIS laid on his right side, facing her in the bed, with his head propped up in his right hand. He quietly watched her sleep, enjoying her measured breathing.

"Good morning," he whispered.

At first, she was a little startled. She wasn't used to waking up with a man in her bed. She also was in strange surroundings in the tree house. There was only one room, but it had a wooden floor. Tree branches with wooden boxes snuggled into them served as a dresser and shelves for KIS's few belongings. The bed was a simple wood frame with a crisscross rope lattice supporting a simple mattress on top. The bed was away from the tree trunk, against the outer wall of the cubicle fashioned with woven branches. Becky slowly relaxed, remembering the events leading up to her joining with this man, "Did you get any more sleep?" she asked, a little afraid to move.

"I slept a bit," he told her carefully."

"We've had a whirlwind courtship," Becky said. "I don't know that much about you, just bits and pieces really. You are still somewhat a mystery to me."

He smiled a gently, answering her, "I'm an orphan. My dad was a hospital pharmacist and my mom was a registered nurse. They were killed in a car crash when I was eight. I was sent to live on my uncle's farm in Lancaster County, Pennsylvania after that."

"That's what Wela said back at the village," Becky agreed. "I take it, you didn't like your uncle? You ran away to join the Marines?"

KIS moved his head, yes and no, "It was OK, but my uncle is very religious, very set in his ways," he explained.

"That lifestyle just wasn't for me. I wasn't allowed to talk to girls; the men and women were pretty much separated all the time, unless you followed very strict rules. Then I joined the Marines, and again I lived my life, mostly among men," he frowned. "I haven't had much female contact in my life, even just to talk," KIS confided.

He rolled on his back, "I felt a large part of my life was lacking," he went on. "Half the world is filled with these other kind of people, girls – women that I know nothing about," he said frustrated. "I'm afraid to touch a lady because I am afraid with my big size, afraid I'll hurt them unintentionally. I prayed for something different," he brightened, "and then you fell into my life. It was as if the spirits answered my prayer, and brought you into my world."

She laughed softly, pulling the sheet a little higher under her chin. With his finger, he gently moved the sheet down as she mockingly protested, "I'll get cold. I'm not wearing a nightgown."

"I know. Your body is so very different than mine. It's so beautiful. I want to learn all about you. I've been granted my wish to be with you," he told her, "you are my goddess."

She touched the side of his face; they moved simultaneously to meet in a morning kiss. In time their lips parted.

"Where was I," she tried to bring her feet back to the ground, "you're distracting me," she gently complained.

"You're such a pleasant distraction," he answered.

"KIS," she turned on her side, in his mirror image, pulled the sheet up above her chest, her head resting on a pillow, with her on her left side, "I was cross-examining you. Learning all your intimate details," she laughed. She gently slapped his hand as he tried to lower the sheet again.

"Oh, is that what you're doing," he laughed with a deep, manly laugh. "I sense the lawyer in you. Is that something you inherited from your disowned mother, I presume?"

"Oh!" she interceded, "you wax poetic do you? Are you a

reader in the romance novel genre? And yes, I inherited some of my mother's good traits," she told him adding, "but I'm careful to filter out her evil inclinations."

"You've found me out, dear princess. I read romance novels in my spare time. Sometimes Owl and I would get into fist-fights with some of my barrack's mates." He laughed, "They called me a fruit."

"Oh! I bet that didn't go down well," she laughed.

KIS moved his head, thinking as he spoke, "It wasn't the sissy part I minded. Marines' joke about all sorts of things and it's part of barrack's or military life. It was the fact that they challenged my maleness, inferring that I was effeminate because I tried to learn how to be romantic. Romance was something I had no clue about. Owl and I'd gotten into some doosies of fights."

"Doosies?" she looked surprised. "Wow, I haven't heard that term since being with my grandparents years ago. They were from the World War II era."

"I spent some time with my grandma too," KIS clarified, "on my dad's side. My mom came from a large family of all older brothers and sisters, they were from the WW II era too. I like that time in history. It was a tragic time with the loss of loved ones in the war, but then again, there was hope for a better life. That period in history makes me feel comfortable. I love the glamour and glitz. Maybe it was the spice of danger that adds color. I could live in those years very easily."

"Wow, that's so cool," she exclaimed, "I loved that time too. The women in their beautiful dresses; their hair fixed signature ways, the makeup was so beautiful. Men dressed in their different style suits were exciting, the Zoot Suiters and the like. Everyone expressed himself or herself differently, but elegantly. Classy was respected, being dirty and ignorant wasn't. The emphasis in life was to strive for something better. Maybe we have things in common after all."

KIS looked at her, "Our meeting and time together might

seem short for us to consider ourselves married," he reflected. "But I remember mom and dad, mom mostly, telling me about couples who got married on a 48 hour pass from the military in World War II, before the soldier was shipped overseas. People judged a potential mate quickly back then. Time was something they didn't have much of. Mom talked to me about how strange it was for a couple to rejoin after the war was over and continue their married life. They knew so little about each other, but they learned as they went through life together. Some made it, others didn't. Does that make sense to you?"

"Yes," she said, "I remember my grandparents talking about the same thing, that not all people have long courtships or engagements. Today, people are too sensible to have whirlwind romances. They might have whirlwind one night stands, but not whirlwind marriages." She confided, "I was attracted to you, oh, after the first hour or so."

Surprised he asked, "It took an hour for my magnetic charm to woo you?"

Laughing, she answered, "Yes, you didn't have me from hello. You were rather beastly at first, not wanting to help me, not wanting to commit," she wrinkled her nose. "I guess it was after you killed that alligator, protected me from all those snakes and killed one. Then you also shot those three men in the airboat and saved me from their evil intentions. Then you shot my tormentor Carlos in the helicopter, but you also taught me how to drive an airboat. That's really when I was yours," she told him with an innocent face. "You gave me freedom with no strings attached.

"You were mine at that point? Wow, you took some effort to win your heart," he laughed. "I didn't know you were mine until you let me kiss you last night at the fire," he told her, smiling, but careful not to lick his lips.

"Girls like to be mysterious," she said shyly, 'didn't you read that in your trashy romance novels?" she asked surprised.

Frowning, "It's the no-no, yes-yes girls that confuse me,"

he admitted. "The right fighting evil thing, I understand that part pretty well."

She smiled, but bumped against his nose with her right index finger, "Your princess is getting hungry. Our romp last night has given me an appetite. I'll have to be careful," she warned, "you can make me fat."

"Do you want to limit our night time romps?" he asked concerned.

She gave him a peck on the lips, "No, I have to watch what I eat after. Easily, I could turn into a refrigerator burglar after our love making, I fear."

She waited a minute, then urged him with widened eyes, "Well, what's for breakfast?" she asked plainly.

He was slapped back into reality, "I wasn't expecting company and hadn't gone to the grocery store lately." He stood up and walked across the room to a cardboard box on the floor, looking down "Let's see what we have to eat."

His bent over to read, distracting her. She wasn't used to this side of a man. He'd forgotten to put his shorts on. He announced without looking back, "We have: beef stew, meat loaf with cheese tortellini, pork chops, chicken with cavatelli, beef with mushrooms ..."

She stopped him, "What ARE you reading?"

"MRE entrees, meals ready to eat, very GI, Government Issue", he answered. "I lived on these for years in the Corp."

"Yup," she was mimicking his deep voice, "done that body good, I can see," she smiled an impish smile. "Hope when you said you liked to cook, that our diet would be more than MREs?" she asked concerned.

He stood up frustrated, looking at her with a scowl on his face. She answered quickly, "I'll have the beef with mushrooms, well done please."

He tossed her the purplish-brown GI pouch as he selected his, "And the maestro will have the chicken and rice pilaf, doused with a generous spritz of hot chipotle sauce and red pepper flakes for extra flavor."

She sat up and started trying to open the thick plastic envelope, but couldn't. Seeing her dilemma he reached over to his pistol belt hanging over a chair and unsheathed his 14-inch bowie knife, "This is why I carry this pig-sticker," he grinned, "that and when I keep gators from eating defenseless naked damsels in the swamp."

"OH? Do you meet many girls in the swamp, that jump naked from airplanes?" she asked, as he showed her how to eat the thing.

"Nope, but the first one I did meet, I married her right off before she could get away or change her mind," he smirked with a raised eyebrow.

"Good answer buster," she said as she smeared some cheese spread on a cracker, standing up, not wanting to get crumbs in their bed.

"Wow," he laughed, "I wish I had my camera."

She glared at him with a squinted eye, not dignifying his statement. She strangely found, that the cheese spread wasn't bad or, was she, that hungry?

"You know KIS," she pointed out, "you owe me a real wedding and a honeymoon too when we get time," she said as she spread more cheese on another cracker.

"In that order?" he wanted to know.

She moved her stance to the other hip, "I'm negotiable," she countered, "Make me an offer," she looked at him full on.

KIS finished his meal and started getting dressed. She sat on the edge of the bed, enjoying her meal and a movie. She spied the wooden box Wela had given to KIS with his mail, yesterday at the fishing village.

"What's in the box?" she asked. "Can I have it when you're through? Looks like it could make a lovely jewelry box, when I get some bling, that is," she hinted.

KIS picked up the box, cut the seal with his ever present, handy-dandy bowie knife, "This is my month's supply of Ashten cigars, hand-rolled beauties."

"Can I have the box when you're done with it?" she asked again.

He took out a punch from his picket, put a hole in the closed end of the tan cigar and fired her up. He savored the rich taste of the thick smoke.

"At least they aren't the stinky cigars, KIS. They're not too bad," she said.

KIS didn't let her off that easy either, "So you like jewelry? You like bling?"

She looked at him, "Very good! You're learning a woman's language."

He grinned, "Not bad for reading Cazmo for three years, eh?"

She jerked, "You read that rag?"

"Well, I wanted to learn about women. It was as close as I could get. I wasn't going to do the twenty-dollar lap-dance circuit," he laughed. I'd have learned the wrong things about women that way.

She walked over to him, as she finished her cheese-cracker, "Maybe I'll have to tutor you, in the finer points of being acceptable to a woman," she whispered, kissing him gently on the nose. "You already know the bling word, that's a start. We'll have to work on your kissing, won't we?"

"What's wrong with my kissing?" he laughingly protested.

She gave him a gentle peck on the lips, "Well you were a little slow at first, but then you got into it. The ending wasn't bad I'll have to admit. I think we'll have to work on all of this. It could get to be a habit of ours."

"You mean cause I didn't give you the tongue?" he asked with a smirk.

She stepped back, "Oh, the tongue thing is very over-rated.

Kissing to me is like a bull-fight," she grinned, imagining, "it's the dancing, the teasing, the building of the passion, then, when the time is right, you stab to the heart."

"Oh, I so understand that," he grinned, "shall we practice now?"

Becky sat back on the bed, "No, you're the hunter. You need to go and hunt for your woman. I'm going to go back to sleep. You kept waking me up all night, you beast you."

KIS smiled a contented smile. She watched this man, her man, get dressed.

He had his long pants on, next his boots, his pistol belt, tying down the holster to his left thigh. He took out a short cylinder and a long metal cylinder from a box on a limb of the tree.

"You said you wanted meat rather than fish?" he asked.

Becky nodded as she turned and slipped under the covers, "Yep."

"I'm going to take the silencers, for my pistol and my rifle," he explained. "I don't want to make noise, to let people know we're here." Almost as an after thought, he took his custom machete down and clipped it to his pistol belt thinking, 'There's just a chance; I might not drop a wild boar in his tracts. If he crawls off into the brush to die, I'll have to hack my way through the saplings and brush to dig him out."

She was starting to drift off, "Sounds nice dear. Go bring home the bacon."

She felt him kiss her lightly on the cheek. Then warm memories of his strong arms holding her snug and secure until she fell asleep, helped her drift off.

KIS walked down to the beach and left the airboat tied up, taking his trusty canoe instead. He wasn't used to being with a woman, especially over night. His mind was on her softness, the smell of her hair. He didn't see the tiny yellow light blinking on the right side of the airboat's engine as he poled away.

He'd remembered seeing some wild boar on an island about five miles to the north where he didn't usually go. He normally preferred fishing. Fish were easier all the way around, easier: to catch, to clean, to cook, and were small enough there weren't leftovers. With the boar, he'd have to smoke or jerk the rest of the carcass. It was a lot work, but wasn't having a woman just that, a lot of work? Something worth having often takes effort.

KIS, made his choice. Love was blossoming between Becky and he. He liked this warm feeling. He'd prayed for years for a woman, to come into his life. He smiled now that his prayers had been answered.

Miles away back on his island, hidden from view by the tall saw grass fields, Becky was fast asleep. KIS had lost view of the island long ago.

Becky was wakened a little while later. She at first tried to ignore her old friend, but she wouldn't be denied.

"Hey, Becky! Give us details," Cathy demanded.

"I want to sleep, Cathy. I'm tired," Becky whined, "besides, it's none of your business," she answered more firmly.

Cathy wouldn't let it slide, "Can't you walk or is that on old wives' tale?"

"Whaa?" Becky gasped, opening one eye.

Cathy became bold, "Is he a Rough Rider or a Tender Prince? Was the hand theory proven out? Does he wear boxers or briefs?"

"You're terrible!" Becky complained hugging her pillow tighter, throwing KIS's pillow over her head, so she couldn't hear Cathy anymore. "Where do you come up with this stuff?"

Cathy giggled, "Well he reads Cazmo, I read Soldier of Fortune. Some of the guys in that magazine could wrestle me down and make me surrender, anytime," she giggled.

There was a silent pause. 'This wasn't like Cathy,' Becky thought. She took the pillow from over her head. She heard an airboat, no, more than one. 'Was it KIS?' she wondered, 'back so soon?'

"Get dressed, Becky. I think we have company!" Cathy said in a strange voice, a voice Becky hadn't heard before.

Becky snuggled down deeper, "I want to sleep, Cath. Leave me alone."

Cathy shouted, "Rebecca Allison, get out of bed and dressed, NOW."

Cathy hadn't used her formal name for many years. Becky got out of bed and dressed in record time. She heard three airboats circling the island. Soon they converged at the beach a few yards out. She could hear the motors idle as masculine voices excitedly chattered. Then the airboat engines stopped. Her blood froze.

"I don't want her harmed, in any way," she heard a man say. "The first man who bruises that package will answer to me! Understand?" the voice shouted.

"Bueno," another man answered.

"OH, Cathy," Becky looked through the branches on the trees, "that's Raul, Raul Mendoza! Where'd he come from?"

"Search the island," Raul ordered. "Someone find her. That homing signal on our airboat couldn't be wrong. She's here somewhere."

"What of that hombre?" another voice questioned. "Someone is with her and he's death on two feet. Diablo himself I'd say."

"I don't care about that vaquero. That's why I brought twelve fierce men with me, or don't you sissies think you can handle one man?" Raul exploded.

From far off a man called, "Senor Mendoza, there's no one on the island."

Almost simultaneously someone shouted, "This looks like a tree house. There's a ladder here."

There was a silent pause. Becky was sure the thumping heart in her chest would give her away.

From directly below her, she heard Raul, "Ah! We meet again in this lifetime, Becky. Please come down." In a moment when there wasn't an answer, he followed with, "I can send a man up to get you, but I don't think that's necessary, do you?"

"The Jig is up!" Cathy gasped, "Like rats in a sinking ship, we can't even jump overboard," she grumbled.

"Will you, hush! They'll hear you. I'm coming down, Raul," Becky replied, "Give me a minute."

Becky climbed down the ladder; dressed in a peasant top, short shorts and her new sneakers. She stood before Raul.

"Whom were you talking to up there," he asked her.

Becky looked embarrassed, "Sometimes I talk to myself. I am alone."

"What about the vaquero who protected you?" Raul asked. He snapped a finger, pointing up in the tree. One of the men jumped to his Jefe's command, climbed the ladder and searched the tree house above.

The man climbed down the ladder and held up the sheet from the bed. Becky felt like they were back in medieval times.

"Jefe, it looks like the chica and her hombre fiesta last night," he grinned showing the other men in the group, who smiled a knowing smile.

Becky put a hand over her heart as Raul took the sheet and examined it, "Is this so? I thought you would remain untouched until your wedding day? That you were so protective of your virtue that you tried to kill yourself, stupidly jumping from the airplane? You've cost me much in men. All of this has strained my friendship with my business associates in Bogotá, who are my family."

Becky didn't say a thing. Raul saw it in her blue eyes.

Raul calmly handed the sheet to one of his man, sighing, "Becky, you've cost me much money too. You're so young, very beautiful, and intelligent. I have a customer waiting in Bogotá, an oriental gentleman, who was willing to pay one hundred thousand dollars for the privilege of being your first. Now all of those plans have been ruined. You've thrown yourself away, for free!"

Becky was appalled, "You speak of very personal matters like so many of your business deals. You're despicable," she spat.

Raul was unfazed, "Of course that's your opinion, not mine. Now, there's the matter of the missing duffle bag, of my money, we were going to drop that night to a waiting fishing trawler in the Gulf of Mexico. It is still unaccounted for. In the duffle bag was one million US dollars. THAT I can get passionate about, senorita," Raul explained with growing anger. "WHERE'S MY MONEY?"

"I don't have it," Becky said flatly. "My man does."

Raul dropped his head, "And where, is your vaquero, now?"

Becky stood still, strangely confident, "He went fishing."

Raul was getting irritated, but he would play her game, "Will he be back for you, or was last night only a drunken party?"

There was ice in her voice, "Oh, I'd say he'll be back. I think you can count on that."

Raul was intrigued, "I have twelve of my best killers here, they're armed to the teeth, but you seem strangely calm. Why is that?" he asked.

Becky looked Raul directly in the eye. Her piercing look sent a chill down his spine, "I hope you understand what you are getting yourself into Raul," Becky said. "If you're stupid enough to harm me, you'll pray for a quick death. I think he can be very lethal if he gets angry and NO, you're twelve assassins WON'T be enough."

Raul shook himself mentally, laughing, showing his macho. He heard Becky. He knew she didn't joke. There wasn't any give in this girl. He chose to be cautious, "Spread the men around the island. We'll wait. He'll be back and when he does, we'll kill him and his slut, after I get my money. Don't anyone fall asleep or you'll answer to me. The chica will stay with me," he shouted to everyone.

KIS had just shot the boar at a distance of 325 yards. 'It's good to keep in practice,' he thought. 'Shots less than that distance are for woosies.'

Suddenly, a vision of the island flashed in his head, followed by the idea, 'better get home,' made his heart skip a beat and ice run in his veins.

KIS turned and left the boar where it laid. He started poling back to the island with firm measured strokes. He was too far away to rush. He hoped Becky was ok. It was almost midday and the sun was overhead. As KIS approached the island, his gaze locked onto a flock of birds who would've landed in a tree on his island, but suddenly veered off. This made KIS pause.

It was if KIS's path was being directed. He had a feeling. He sensed a presence, something very familiar, "Owl? Are you with me buddy? Are you here with me now?" he said to the wind and water, but there was only silence.

KIS was directed to glass the island with his rifle scope. He was nearly a thousand yards out. That would be a long shot for a 7.62 mm round. He needed to get closer, especially with Becky on the island. Killing men who had her would be easy, but saving her from their retaliation, called for close in fighting.

He carefully poled to within four 400 yards of the island and stepped on the bank of the canal. He took his sniper M-14 with him and carefully screwed the silencer onto the rifle.

KIS had a theory he wanted to try. He corkscrewed his arm through the leather shoulder strap to give him stability to make his shot. The magazine fed M-14 felt as light as a feather, with the balanced smoothness of the 1903 Springfield.

His rifle was like an extension of his arm. He carefully located three men. He was left handed, so he started on his left.

KIS put the cross hairs of his scope on the forehead of the first man. "Tic" was the sound the rifle made as he fired his first shot, the metallic sound as the bolt stripped the fired casing from the M-14's receiver and rammed a live round into the chamber. "Tic, Tic," two more shots fired close together sounded like a, "Tic – Tic – Tic," and three men sprawled dead in macabre poses.

KIS nodded. His theory was right. With an unsilenced shot, the report caused a soldier to dive for cover and hug the ground. KIS felt that a silenced shot, that blew the head off a companion, would strangely make the survivors pop up instinctively by human nature. It was like cars on a freeway passing a traffic accident. People not affected by the accident HAVE TO see. They don't know what's going on so they pop their heads up to see what happened.

KIS saw two men paired together. He looked through his scope as his trigger finger flexed. 400 yards away the man on the left, the right side of his head disappeared like an exploding melon, whipping his body to the right, his finger instinctively squeezed the trigger on his machine pistol in the throws of death, and stitched his buddy with a long burst of 9 mm rounds.

Finally, the cavalry arrived. KIS had been counting on this. 'The smell of death attracted them,' he knew.

A small man, hiding behind a log, felt something cross his back, and he was stunned to see a large head of a snake, looking down at him! Both snake and man blinked. Then Edward drove his head under the right arm of the man lying in the ground who was screaming his head off, but then his scream choked off as the air was squeezed from his lungs.

As in all situations, there is the unexpected. One fella had to go, he had the call of nature that couldn't be quickly answered, but he was in luck. He'd seen the dilapidated outhouse close to the water. He thought it was strange, but the back of the outhouse was missing. Further thoughts about the building were cut off due to the urgency of his call.

The hit man dropped his drawers and sat on the throne, immediately feeling a sense of relief BUT was short lived due to a deep growl emanating from behind him. His scream faded as he was dragged out the back of the building towards the brown water of the canal. George, the twenty foot ancient alligator had arrived at the party. The man in the outhouse was his hors devours.

KIS put his rifle carefully in the bottom of the boat, and silently poled toward the island. About a hundred yards out, he slipped over the side to swim the distance. He chose the northern side of the island, since Edward was already full and was probably letting his prey settle in his stomach.

KIS drew his machete, the ¼ inch plate steel that has been ground to look like a mini sword and sharper than a razor, from his pistol belt in the water before he came ashore. Shooting people outright had its place, but these men were professionals. They followed the code of a warrior. KIS decided to follow the rules of close combat, face to face.

Movement from his right caught KIS's eye. Silently, he floated like a mist over the island floor to stand just behind the enemy. KIS had a sense of humor as he tapped the killer on his left shoulder. The man swung in the direction of the tap, he faced KIS, their eyes locked before the pistol in his right arm could swing around. His arm was outstretched in natural arch.

KIS had the man's eyes locked with his, as KIS swung his machete in his left hand down on the gun arm of the assassin, surgically severing the man's arm that flopped to the ground. KIS completed his move as he swung the machete in a J movement. With one powerful swing, KIS chopped off the man's head. The headless body hit the damp ground with a wet splat.

Four men remained. One man saw KIS behead his associate, but noticed that KIS had a pistol easily at hand. That KIS had chosen the machete over the woosie pistol was not missed. This was a challenge to a warrior. The man obliged KIS with face-to-face combat. It was a matter of moi macho.

Three other men saw the first man pull his knife, preparing to do battle. It amazed them that KIS had the stones to seek them out, to challenge them to close in fighting. This stranger was an hombre. KIS dropped the machete. He stood ready to fight them bare handed as his nostrils flared with cold anger.

The first man lunged at KIS, his knife arm thrusting at KIS in a professional way with a flick of the razor sharp blade at the end. KIS blocked the knife away from his body with a counter clockwise sweep of his right arm across his body. With his left hand, KIS caught the man's head in his hand and bringing up his right hand, twisted the man's head in one sturdy twist, breaking his neck. The assassin dropped to the ground with the plop of warm cow manure.

Two men working as a team approached KIS next, with a frontal attack, but KIS moved fast, blocking the knife arm of the man on the right side. KIS jammed two outstretched fingers on KIS's right hand into the eye sockets of the assassin on the left, leaving him blinded, defenseless, and on his knees.

KIS reverse swung-stepped to his left and brought the heel of his combat boot up then down on the kneecap of the second assassin who had thrust the knife. The assailant's kneecap popped off, dropping the assassin to his knees in pain. KIS drew his pig-sticker and unceremoniously slit the throat of the man on the right and the left slaughterhouse style.

The final assassin standing now facing KIS was practical. He'd just seen three very capable associates killed with such professionalism he was stunned. Without a moment's hesitation, he shucked his pistol, but had a splitting headache as KIS threw the knife in his hand at the last assassin and sunk the blade almost to the hilt in the forehead of the last hitman.

KIS was really angry now. Raul clearly saw KIS's anger. Raul pulled Becky close his side and put the barrel of his nickel-plated pimp pistol to her skull, "Come any closer, hombre, and I'll blow her brains out," he warned.

KIS was tired, but his veins were filled with adrenaline and moved toward Raul in a very purposeful way, "You kill her, and you'll die, I PROMISE you that," KIS calmly told Raul. "You don't have enough lead in that popgun to stop me."

Raul knew this was true. He'd seen a fatally injured man filled with adrenaline; with twenty bullet holes in him, still kill his assassin. Did he feel lucky?

KIS sensed the beast, "You're a business man. Killing her won't profit you at all, but it will cause your death."

'Ah,' Raul thought. 'Maybe I can reason with him,' "Where's my duffle bag? Where's my money?" he demanded.

"I hid it," KIS said flatly. "Will you trade the girl for the money?"

This time it was Raul, who smiled, "You are a very dangerous man amigo. To have a man such as you on my back trail, I think would be a mistake."

KIS said confidently, "To kill you, if you've haven't harmed my woman, wouldn't profit me," looking Raul straight in the eye.

"You are a business man after all?" Raul wondered aloud.

KIS relaxed, "When you have something I want, yes."

"You want her that bad?" Raul laughed lightly, careful not to offend.

KIS blinked, "She is MY WOMAN," he told Raul seriously.

Raul raised his eyebrows to acknowledge KIS's reply. 'Every man is different', he knew. 'Every man had his price', "Where's my money?" he said.

KIS motioned with his left hand, "Over there. In a hole for safe keeping."

Raul waved the gun towards the hole. KIS moved over to the void, kneeled down at the rim. The hole was only about fourteen inches around. The sun had moved and it was hard to see as the darkness grew under the shading branches of the mangroves.

Raul carefully dragged Becky over to the hole, as he looked down. He saw the familiar green, "Reach down an get it," he told KIS.

KIS looked through smokey eyes, "It's your money. You get it yourself. But I warn you, if you hurt my woman, I'll take you straight to hell," he vowed.

Becky protested, "KIS don't give him the money! I know you can kill him, DO IT. The money is our life," she pleaded.

KIS looked at Raul. Raul knew that KIS could kill him easy, but KIS looked at Becky, "Honey, I was dead until you came into my life. You give me reason to live, the hope to experience life anew. Without you, I don't want to breathe. I asked you to grow old with me, and I meant it. The spirits brought us together." As an after thought KIS told her, "Owl's out there."

Raul panicked, "There's more of you out there?" afraid of the unknown.

KIS's eyes never flickered, "My partner is out there with a scoped weapon. If I don't signal him, you won't leave this island alive."

'This new fact put a whole new spin on things,' Raul felt. Motioning with the pistol "Put your arm down there to show me you haven't booby-trapped it."

KIS's right arm was bare; he'd only had his t-shirt on. He started to put his hand in the hole, but there was a buzzing sound, like an insect, coming from somewhere.

Becky's eyes widened, she knew that sound! "KIS don't. Please don't darling." She had to say it, "I can't live without you either. You've grown on me, you beast you," she cried desperately.

KIS kept his eye squarely on Raul as he put his entire arm down the hole. The buzzing sound stopped, but started up again when KIS removed his arm.

Raul saw that KIS was unaffected, now pushed Becky toward KIS, "Here take her, but you two stand over there away from me. Remember I can still shoot you," he warned.

KIS and Becky hugged each other as Raul started to put his arm down the hole, but stopped, asking, "What's that buzzing sound?"

KIS waved around at the trees, "Bees. I'd recommend you grab the bag and get out of here before they decide to sting you."

Raul didn't wait any longer as he thrust his bare arm down the hole. He flinched as KIS threw Becky and he behind a fallen log.

Raul looked down and saw the two small fang marks as he kneeled on the ground beside the hole. His worst fears were confirmed. Raul felt himself lose control, due to his deathly fear of snakes. Spiders and snakes had been Raul's worst nightmare, his largest fear in life. Now that he'd been bitten by the deadliest rattler in the Everglades, he started to tremble uncontrollably and seize, although his least memory in this life, was this Beast and his beauty, staring at him as his vision clouded and he plunged into his hellish reward.

KIS and Becky looked at each other. KIS was amazed his plan had gone better than he'd hoped. KIS got up, kneeled down, and checked Raul's body.

"Is he dead, KIS?" Becky asked nervously with her arms nervously crossed over her chest.

"I'd say so," KIS replied without emotion.

Becky flung herself against KIS in a fearful embrace, "Are you alright? Did that pigmy rattler bite you too?"

KIS held up his arm and showed her the twin fang marks.

"Are you crazy?" she screamed.

KIS looked into her eyes, "Yes girl, I'm crazy about you."

Becky complained, "Our life together will be short, if you die of snakebite like Raul over there," she nodding gestured.

KIS was starting to feel woozie, so he walked away from Raul. KIS sat down against a root looking at Becky; "Up in the tree house there's a gray Styrofoam container with a phone taped to it. Get it, please," he told her.

Becky ran to the ladder and in a second, came back with the box. KIS untapped a satellite phone, and punched in a number,

"Hello Chris? This is KIS," he nodded, "yep, I got bit by a pigmy rattler about twenty-seven inches long. Yup a pretty good sized one. What?" laughing KIS said, "I'm not sure I can save it for you. Yes, ok, six vials in 250 mls of saline over two hours. Thanks for the help."

Becky could only hear half the conversation, "Who was that? What's in the box?"

KIS opened the box; half the Styrofoam box had IV bags, needles, and clear vials of liquid. The other half was sealed. KIS broke the seal and a cloud of smoke came out.

"Antivenom," KIS explained, "Its kept refrigerated in dry ice."

KIS went to work, reconstituting the vials, and then he sucked the antivenom from the vials with a syringe, injected it into an IV bag, put a needle attached to IV tubing in a vein in his right arm and started infusing the lifesaving drug into his body.

KIS looked at Becky finally, "I've been working with Dr. Chris Swenson, a herpetologist from the state university over the last year. I collect poisonous snakes for him, and we milk them for their venom. The drug companies make antivenom to save lives. This keeps me in cigar money," he grinned.

This gave Becky an idea. She ran to the tree house and brought back a cigar. KIS lit it and puffed away happy as a clam.

KIS told Becky, "Chris is a medical doctor also and told me how much antivenom I needed, for the size of snake that bit me. I've been bitten before and Chris was getting tired of flying way out here to save me, so he came up with this idea. It wasn't a bad idea either," he said. Thinking out loud, "Not all venomous snake bites, like the pigmy rattler, which is the most poisonous snake in the Glades, inject venom into his prey every time it bites," he explained.

"Did Raul die from the venom?" Becky asked.

KIS looked over at Raul, "No, I don't think so. I think it could've been a freak allergic reaction, or he just got so scared, his heart gave out."

After that, things went blank for KIS.

Chapter 13

KIS slowly opened his eyes. He saw Becky anxiously sitting next to him on the bed. 'The light was dim, so it must be morning?' he wondered.

"What happened?" KIS asked Becky.

"Are you alright?" she asked him worriedly, "don't you remember?"

KIS tried to sit up, but his head started to throb and generally felt like a mule had kicked him, "Whoa, I guess I'd better lay flat for a bit," he said.

Becky got up and started to change into clean clothes, "OH KIS, you gave me a fright. Don't you remember any of last night?

KIS propped his arm under his head enough to look at her while she changed. She was sooo different than he. He marveled every time he saw her.

"KIS!" she stamped her foot, "Are all men as lecherous as you?" She wanted to hear his answer.

KIS shrugged innocently, "You're just so beautiful. You take my breath away," he confessed.

She finished dressing. It felt good to be in clean clothes again. 'Yesterday had been horrible,' she thought, 'but at least people won't be chasing them now, or was she mistaken about that too?'. "KIS, tell me what you remember about yesterday. You told me to ask you, last night."

"I'm better after a cup of coffee," he grinned.

"Oooooooo," she stamped her foot, "Are all men so aggravating?" she gasped annoyed. "Ok, I'll help you down stairs." She didn't see his smiling face.

KIS threw back the covers and sat up, "WOW, that isn't such a good idea," he said as the room spun around him.

She pushed him back into bed, sitting up, leaning against the headboard, "You tell me what you want, and I'll try to get it, OK?"

"We don't have to go downstairs to the fire pit, Becky," he explained. "I have a plastic jug of water, a metal GI cup, and a holder on the shelf. In the box of MREs, is a packet of coffee, and a heat tablet, see it?" he asked.

Becky found all the things he described. She set up the contraption and heated the water.

"Now dump the coffee powder into the cup and stir it with one of the plastic spoons in the MRE box," he directed. "Do you like cream and sugar in your coffee?" he wondered. He was learning about her too.

"It depends," she told him. "Sugar and cream are fattening, even with skim milk, which makes the best cappuccino, or café con leche." She smiled coyly with her eyes, "and a girl as to watch her figure."

KIS's eyes were on her. He slowly nodded as he drank in all of her.

"But I'll drink the coffee today, any way you want it," she answered.

KIS became a bit serious, "GI coffee in the packet is pretty raw, so better put two creams and three sugars in please. I love good coffee, but today I can't be choosey," he told her.

She did as he directed, handed him the cup, and as he drank, she said a little more relaxed, "I'm glad you like good coffee. I do too. Another thing we have in common. So far, we're on the positive side in our match made by the spirits."

Over the cup he eyed her, "Other than I'm so aggravating?" he smiled.

She squared her shoulders, hands on her hips; "Yes, you certainly are aggravating at times," she answered, a little softly, trying to hold back a smile. She was amazed how much she appreciated his company already.

KIS took a good pull on the coffee, then handed her the

cup. He marveled at how daintily she sipped the coffee. Her movements, everything about her intrigued him.

"I remember the fight yesterday," he recalled. "Oh wow!" he remembered, "I think Owl was with me when I was coming back to the island to get to you. It was like, he was moving me to see targets, but he didn't say anything. He just gave me pictures in my head. It was weird, but I did feel his presence. It was like old times, us working together."

She sat on the side of the bed, handing the cup back to him. He looked over the rim of the coffee cup at her, "Coffee in the morning always goes better with a cigar," he said slowly.

She looked at him sarcastically, "You're starting to get pushy," she said, 'or was he just getting used to her, and he was being himself?'

He gave her a little boy look. "Ok, OK," she sighed. She walked over to the wooden box of cigars, took one out, slid it from of the plastic wrapper, sniffed the tobacco, "mmmm they always smell so good before you light them," she marveled. "You'll have to tell me how to do this for you. How to prepare the master's cigar," she smiled. She had to admit she liked caring for him, doing little things to please him. He was so different than her, so animal.

KIS showed her. She watched how he carefully lit it.

After a few puffs he went on, "I remember talking with Raul, getting bit by the snake, tricking him into putting his arm down the hole, him getting bit, and then him dying. I remember calling Chris Swenson on the satellite phone and getting the directions for making the antivenin IV. That's about it," he recalled.

"You don't remember calling Chris back? You said your arms were starting to tingle and getting stiff?" she asked worriedly.

"Nope," he answered.

"Chris told you to mix up some lorazepam in a syringe, to get to a bed where you could sleep, and push the solution into the IV line. You told me to take the IV line out of your arm when you were asleep. Do you remember any of that?" she asked.

"Nope," he answered, but not surprised. "Lorazepam makes you forget what happened in the last 24 hours. It's called retrograde amnesia."

"How do you know all this, this medical stuff?" she asked.

KIS sat up feeling better, after drinking the coffee. He tried to stand up, wobbled a little, but staggered over to his pants, "Our unit in the Corp was a behind the lines' outfit. We were usually all alone, real sneaky pete stuff. We didn't have the support services regular field units had. Owl and I were trained as medics, corpsman. They trained us so well; we could perform moderate surgery in the field, with help over the radio, like what happened yesterday with Chris. We did stuff like that all the time."

"I don't mean to be ghastly," she hesitated, "but what do we do with the bodies of the hit men now? Those men laying dead down there, is giving me the gibblies."

KIS took a long pull on the cigar, blew out a huge puff of smoke and grinned, "Did you ever hear of gator bate?"

"You're not," she looked shocked.

"You can bet your bootie," KIS answered firmly, "and there's no trace," he smiled. "That's what I'm gonna do. You can stay here if you want. The ride out can be unpleasant, but I've smelled it before. Some chopper rides from the battlefield can be horrifying, even with the dead in body bags," he remembered.

"Oh no! You're not leaving me alone again. I'm coming with," she told him, following him down the tree house ladder close on his heals.

"Stay here," he told her as he started picking up bodies, throwing them over his shoulder like a sack of feed, and carrying them down to the biggest airboat they had. Before he made his second trip, he went over each boat with a fine tooth comb. Then he walked back to the camp where she waited for him.

"I found a homing device on each of the four boats," he told her, passing by for another body.

"What do we do with them," she asked, sitting on a stone by the fire pit.

KIS hefted the body without the head. He didn't bat an eye as he picked the man's severed head by the hair, and with the body draped over his right shoulder, he continued on with his chore, "I smashed 'em. I don't want any more guys following us. I'm getting tired of killing them, and eventually I'm gonna make a mistake. Then that'll be the end of us."

It gave her a shiver, "And then we'll be the gator bate ourselves, right?"

KIS nodded his head solemnly, "I'm thinking we need to get outa here," he told her, looking around, "I don't think we're safe in the Glades any more."

Quickly, he finished loading all the bodies from the island, remembering Edward got one guy and George got another. KIS stopped by the fire pit to relight his cigar.

Becky looked like she wanted to say something. KIS asked, "Wha?"

"I've been thinking," she said, as her thoughts formed in her head, "We now have two million dollars, in cash, in duffle bags, in the US."

KIS blew out a puff of smoke, "Yep, sounds right."

"Well, in America these days you can't just walk into a bank with that much cash and not get a visit from the feds real quick," she explained.

"Ooo," KIS sat up, "good thinking girl. That's what I like, a team effort."

She furthered her idea, explaining, "We can't deposit the money in the US. We can't go through an airline either to get to another country, because they x-ray the bags now in the airports. We'll get caught."

KIS sat down, "You said we couldn't deposit the money in the US? What about a foreign country? How about Cuba?"

She thought for a moment, "Cuba won't work since we don't have diplomatic relations with that country, we couldn't get in," she frowned, "but good idea." In a minute she questioned, "How would you've gotten us to Cuba?"

KIS beamed the biggest smile, "I have my graduation project yonder."

"I don't understand. Tell a poor city girl, in plain English," she told him.

KIS stood up like he was going to give a presentation, "Well you know, I was almost finished my Mechanical Engineering Degree, and I have an interest in flying. I had to complete a mechanical engineering project and turn it into the college to graduate."

"I'm on pins and needles here, KIS, give!" she shook her hands.

Rather than tell her, KIS took her hand and walked down one of the sandy paths, like a spoke on a wheel, down to the water. The hub of the island was the tree house. He led her to a green canvas tarp and pulled it off, "Ta-Da."

"What IS THAT," Cathy piped up? "Tell me it's not what I think it is!"

"Ok," Becky hesitated, "this is a toy airplane sitting on pontoon floats?"

KIS looked hurt, "No it's not. It's a work of art. I got it as a kit and put it together myself, right here. I was going to fly it to Cuba and get 100 pounds of cigars for my graduation present. I just haven't had the time yet."

"That looks like a death trap to me," Cathy grumped.

"Don't be so negative," Becky answered above and to the right. Becky stood a little bolder answering KIS's questioning look, "I stand up for you, no matter what Cathy says about you, KIS," she nodded her head decidedly.

KIS went on, "This, is the Flaming Eagle. There's: aluminum D cell wing construction with aluminum wing ribs, with 4130 chromoly steel tubing fuselage, cub style bungee cord suspension system, and in cabin adjustable elevator trim."

Becky looked at the plane, "Where's the gas tank?"

KIS pointed just in front of the cabin, "See the cap with the hooked wire from a coat-hanger, coming out of it, see?"

"What's the wire for," Becky was afraid to ask.

KIS casually answered, "Oh, that's the fuel gauge. The wire is stuck in a cork that floats in the gasoline," adding, "when the hook on the wire meets the cap on the fuel tank, we're out of gas."

"We're gonna Crash and Burn!" Cathy moaned.

Becky shook off her negative friend, "I'm starting to get into this," she smiled and wiggled her head, "a little crazy, but it might just work. Go on, tell me more."

"There's side by side seating in a 44 inch wide cabin, I'd call cozy," he smiled, "Passenger doors can be opened and closed in flight, gull wing style engine compartment covers, duel stick and rudder controls, throttle system on the port bulkhead, large baggage area behind the seats, and a large windscreen for excellent visibility. Wingspan is 33 feet 6 inches, a ten-gallon gas tank; overall length is 20 feet 6 inches. I have the 65 hp engine, with electric start. Our cruise speed would be 60 miles per hour, stall speed is about 35 mph, we'll burn 4 gallons of gas per hour, so we have a range of about 150 miles before the hook hits the fuel cap," he took a breath.

Becky blinked. She knew what that meant.

KIS could see Becky was thinking, "Wha?"

"We can't go to Cuba, but what about Freeport in the Bahamas?" she wondered aloud.

KIS did some math in his head. Then with a funny look to his face, "I think we can make that."

"It's either yes or no!" Cathy interjected. "I'm not going for a swim in the Atlantic Ocean thank you," she added in a huff.

'Don't get your knickers in a knot,' Becky told Cathy. Turning with a smile Becky asked KIS, "We'd like a more definite answer please. Can we make it to Freeport? Yes or No?"

KIS looked at her, but he still had that funny smile on his face, "Yes."

Cathy wailed "He's saying Yes-Yes, but there's No-No in his eyes!"

Becky was a mirror image of his answer, 'Yes. You see, Cathy,' she thought, 'he says we can make it. And I believe him. See he survived that rattler bite yesterday. Go back to sleep, I'm handling this,' as Cathy grumbled away.

"When could we go?" Becky asked KIS.

Holding up a finger, he took the phone and called the flight service station in Miami, "What's the weather look like for a flight from Fort Lauderdale to Freeport this week?" he asked.

Becky could only hear the one sided conversation. She sat patiently.

"Great! Tomorrow morning, Friday, sounds fine, almost nonexistent winds if we leave early, and bright sunshine. Thanks for your help," he signed off.

Becky looked at him, "Can that phone call Freeport from here?"

Nodding, "Yep. These phones link to ComSat, the communications satellite overhead so we don't need a tower like most cell phones do. Why?"

"I want to call the Freeport Yacht Club," she answered calmly.

He laughed, protesting, "But you don't know the number."

Becky smiled, "I've a photographic memory. I'm not just another pretty face ya-know," she smirked. "I spent a whole gloomy spring in the Chicago Public Library reading." Proudly, she added, "I've read the whole World Encyclopedia. It was a magnificent read. So clearly explained," she reminisced.

"Ok smarty," KIS tested her, "Who's the winning pitcher in the 1938 Baseball World Series?"

Becky looked up and efforted, "The 1938 Baseball World Series was between the New York Yankees and the Chicago Cubs. New York won the world series, four games to none. It says is that the starting pitcher, Red Ruffing, won two games, but his pitch to hit average stunk," she nodded back at him.

KIS laughed, "I'm impressed! Maybe we can't loose."

Becky daintily picked up the phone and dialed. When there was an answer, she asked to speak to the Freeport Yacht Club manager. This time it was KIS, who could only hear half the conversation.

"Yes, hello, this is Mrs. Swoboda. No, you don't know me, but my husband, and I would like to join your club," she covered the phone asking KIS, "Do you have a credit card? And does it have a $ 5,000 limit?" she asked.

KIS nodded yes answering her, but also had a feeling this was a harbinger of things to come. He handed her his credit card. 'Wow,' he thought, 'what an amazing girl.'

Armed with her plastic, Becky was ready to do battle. She rattled off the card number.

"Marvelous," she continued, "We so appreciate you taking our membership application over the phone. And what is your name please? Mor-reece? It's nice to meet you, Morrice. We'd also like to reserve the Honeymoon Suite, yes the one overlooking the harbor of course. My husband and I will be flying in from the mainland tomorrow morning, yes Friday." She added, "We want to start a business in Freeport.

Are there any Swiss Banks in town? Oh yes, I know them. You say Siegfried Henkle is the Director of New Accounts? I look forward to us having a long and profitable relationship, Morrice. Yes, cherro."

"I'm truly impressed Becky! You're wonderful," KIS complimented her.

She dialed one more number, "I have one more call to make," she grinned. Oh, how she loved this. She was on familiar ground now.

"Herr Henkle please, in new accounts. Yes, I'll hold," Becky moved her feet in the dirt waiting. Finally, "Yes, Herr Henkle, I'm Mrs. Swoboda from the US. My husband and I would like to open a new account with your bank. We'd like to start a company in Freeport, an investment corporation really, just a moment," she stopped.

KIS interjected, "I might want to dabble in some salvage too, later."

Becky, without missing a beat, "We might want to start a salvage branch of our business in time. We want to bring our initial deposit with us tomorrow morning; will you be in around noon? We'll be bringing cash in US currency."

There was a long pause as Becky listened, "No, Herr Henkle. We got the money in a fire hall bingo game, all two million dollars."

KIS blinked at this special little woman who'd just fallen into his life. He was amazed at her business savvy and assertiveness.

Becky listened again, grinning, "You get the idea Herr Henkle. Discretion is a must, but no, we aren't into drugs, and no we don't dabble in white slavery. We leave that to other companies. We have no interest in those kinds of operations. Yes, it's a deal. Ok, then noon on Friday it is. We might be a little before or after. We're flying in from the States." She looked worriedly between KIS and their experimental kit airplane, "our arrival will be dependent on the wind. Good-bye."

Becky sat back, "Ok, I did my part. Now all you have to do is get us there."

KIS smiled, "I have a good feeling about us. I get us where we want to go, and you make all the other arrangements. Works for me."

Becky held out her hand. They shook hands and sealed it with a kiss.

Becky wrinkled her nose as she remembered, "We still have those bodies to get rid of."

KIS scurried into the tree house and got two more MREs, "One more day of these meals, but I hope in Freeport, we can have something more tasty."

In short order, KIS dropped off the thirteen bodies in a twenty-mile radius of the island. He was careful not to dump them all in one place so not to cause the gators' indigestion. Human's can be a little rich and might give the alligators' gas.

Next he took the airboat back to the island, where he tied one boat to the back of his airboat and the remaining boat to the airboat Becky drove. KIS led the way back to the fishing village and Wela's general store. When they were tying up the boats, the ever-present Pima appeared. Wela, after hearing about their last meeting was quick to show up, to referee any dispute.

KIS whispered to Becky, who nodded, "Pima," KIS said, "Becky, and I'd like to give you these three airboats. We found them floating empty and abandoned south of here, as a gift from the spirits. We'll keep the first one, we got. You'll need to paint the other three boats tribal colors and disguise them a bit," he winked. "Use them to start a tourist business. Show people around the Glades. It's a peace offering from us to you."

"I'll think about it," he grumbled and then walked away deep in thought.

"That was very kind of you, KIS and Becky. We could certainly use the money," Wela was being honest. Some of the village wants to raise funds through casino gambling, but I like old fashioned work, to earn money. But, that's my opinion. The airboats can be another source of income for the village.

"We need some things, Wela, at the general store. We need two suitcases at least," KIS told her.

Wela turned, with an arm around Becky, "Let's go see if you like what I have. We have several different sizes."

They bought two suitcases no longer than forty inches. After a dinner of swamp cabbage with turtle, garfish and pork stew, KIS bought ten gallons of gasoline in cans. Then he and Becky were on the canal heading home before dark.

They put their money carefully in the two new suitcases and headed to bed. It'd been a busy day. Becky fell asleep as soon as she put her head on the pillow.

KIS rummaging around in the tree house just after dawn woke her, "Did you get any sleep?" she asked.

"Not much," he confessed. "I'm always a little jumpy the night before a mission."

Becky sat up in bed, "Are you nervous about the flight? You've flown before, right?"

KIS looked at her, "Honestly, I've flown before, but not in a plane like this. There's always the unknown. Always something unexpected can happen, like before, like with Owl. I said I'd get us there, and I will. But, as I said before, we might live a short but illustrious life."

Becky got out of bed, threw her arms around his neck, and kissed him, "What more can a woman ask for? Nothing ventured, nothing gained."

Becky got dressed. KIS handled the two suitcases and put them into the plane as it rested on its pontoons.

"Pretty handy to have the pontoons to float on the water," she commented.

KIS admired his plane, "Yes, she's a beauty. I wanted a

Lake-6, an amphibious plane with retractable landing gear, so we could land on water or land, but this was all I could afford at the time. She'll have to do for now."

KIS showed Becky how to climb into the copilot's seat (on the right). She almost had to shimmy her way into the seat on her back from the rear of the plane. "Wow, this is uncomfortable!" she groaned. "We'll have to change this way of travel quick. Does the Lake-6 have more room?" she asked.

"Yep, sure does," he said.

Becky thought as KIS climbed into the narrow seat to her left, "We'll have to put a new airplane on our wish list, as soon as our money clears," she said aloud.

KIS nodded, but he was concentrating on the preflight inspection. Then he flipped on the magneto switches and pushed the starter. The propeller whirled and finally caught. As the engine steadied down, he did his engine run up, testing first the left and then the right magneto, rpm drop within normal limits, gas is good, controls free."

"KIS," Becky looked around nervous, "we're moving!"

KIS nodded, "That's normal hon. We're on water not land. There's no brake and the propeller is pulling us forward. I've thought about that," he reassured her.

KIS kicked left rudder to turn the plane into the channel of a long straight canal, "The trouble is," he said, "we're overloaded and might have trouble getting off the ground. Once we're airborne, we're golden," he told her, speaking over the engine noise.

KIS reached over and buckled Becky in with the seatbelt, giving it one generous tug, making her, "Umph."

"My girdle when I was thirteen, wasn't this tight," she smiled at him.

He gave her a blank look, not knowing what she was talking about but then told her, "Better too tight. It might be a bumpy ride at first."

He pushed in full throttle and the little engine started to

scream, as Becky's heart started to pound in her chest. They were racing down the canal, unable to break the suction from the water to get airborne.

"WE'RE GONNA DIE," Cathy screamed as an island ahead kept getting bigger and bigger in their windshield. They had passed the point of no return.

KIS was calm as a cucumber on the outside, but he was starting to sweat. They were running out of canal, 'Oh God, give us some help,' he prayed.

As if a hand directed his head, he spied what looked like a log across the canal. The trouble was the log was moving.

Becky leaned forward, straining her eyes to see what it was, "What's that in the water ahead?" she gasped.

KIS was intent on what he was doing. He shoved in all the throttle the tiny experimental plane had, and bore down on the log.

"KIS, you're going to hit that log across the canal," Becky warned, bracing herself for impact.

He didn't respond. The log got closer and closer.

"OH MY GOD, ITS AN ALLIGATOR," Cathy screamed.

Right at the last minute, KIS pulled back a touch on the yoke, which lifted the nose of the plane up and then, "THUMP," they all were squashed into their seats, and were thrown upward, like flying up off a water-ski ramp. KIS wiggled the yoke to make sure, they were flying, kicked a little left rudder just as the island passed under their right wing. They were airborne!

Becky slapped his right arm, "That was too close!" she cried.

"Whaa? What's your problem?" he looked surprised.

A little put off, Becky asked, "Is that how you fly? Where'd they teach you to use gators as ramps?"

KIS looked sheepish, "No, I haven't flown a plane as underpowered as this one before. I also hadn't counted on your weight plus the money, but you're certainly prettier than a hundred pounds of cigars," he grinned trying to make light of what just happened.

She jerked, "You mean you haven't flown this plane before? Ever?"

KIS smiled, "There's a first time for everything."

"Stop the bus!" Cathy complained, "I need a fresh pair of panties."

He banked left, heading east. He kept low, maybe 300 feet saving on fuel, but over the houses, he had to go up to 1500 feet. He flew a plotted course and was relieved when his dead reckoning navigation proved right. A large island grew in their windshield as the hook in the fuel gauge started to rest on the top of the gas cap.

"Woosh," he exhaled, relieved.

Becky looked worriedly, "Wha?"

He grinned, "I wasn't exactly sure where Freeport was. I don't have any electronic navigation onboard, no radio beacon to fly to. This was all fly by the seat of your pants stuff. Heck, we only have six instruments in this plane. This is old crop duster flying style," he explained to her.

Becky wiped the perspiration off her brow, "Memo to self, add electronic navigation systems to our next plane, already on wish list."

KIS spied the cluster of yachts in a protected cove. He saw the windsock on the roof of the clubhouse, flew downwind and turned the tiny plane into the wind for landing. He kissed the waves and did a perfect landing, turning off the engine just before he beached their plane.

A constable in immaculate white uniform approached them as KIS was helping Becky separate herself from their little bird. KIS turned around to greet the policeman with Becky still in his arms. He put her down gently.

"Good morning, folks," the policeman came to attention,

saluting, "I'm Constable Henderson. And may I ask what brings you to our fair island?"

A man in a 1930's black coat and gray trousers hurried to greet them, "Oh, Freddie old chap. So lovely of you to greet these people for me," he tried to catch his breath. "Their arrival was precipitous. You caught me off guard, but no worries. I haven't learned your eccentricities yet, being new members, what?"

"Morrice," Constable Henderson turned, "you KNOW these people?"

KIS saw two bellhops running toward them, "I'll hang onto the bags, thanks," he told Morrice, who quietly waved the bellhops off.

"As you wish, Mr. Swoboda," Morrice answered. Turning to the policeman, he answered, "Oh yes, Freddie, these folks are new members of our club. The start of a long and fruitful friendship, I hope, what? They have a meeting with Siegfried Henkle at the Swiss Bank. He called to confirm your meeting early this morning, Mrs. Swoboda."

"Constable Henderson, this is HQ, Over," crackled Freddie's radio.

Freddie depressed the talk button on the handset clipped to his shoulder strap, "HQ, Constable Henderson, tally-ho."

"Constable," the female dispatcher continued, "there's a disturbance at the fisherman's wharf, that requires your attention, when you've completed your current assignment. Some sailor's began celebrating with some grog, but the shark they hooked earlier, strangely came back to life and bit off one of the poor sailors' hand. There are all sorts of excitement with that bloodbath, OVer."

Constable Henderson's monocle fell out of his eye as he answered the dispatcher, "We are under control here. I'll proceed to the wharf straight away."

Constable Henderson, saluted crisply, did an about-face,

and briskly marched to his auto and motored off. Everyone breathed a sigh of relief.

Becky extended her hand, "Oh Morrice, my faith in you has been confirmed. You are resourceful and very helpful."

KIS kept silent. He was a fish out of water here. He sensed he should let his tigress handle things. She was in her urban jungle now.

"Would you like to freshen up before your meeting?" Morrice asked.

Becky looked at KIS then back, "No, a car please. We'd like to get our meeting over, and then we can retire to the honeymoon suite. I'm so looking forward to a long soak. I understand you have a first-rate spa here?"

Morrice motioned a man over, whispered instructions into his ear. Then he turned to Becky, "Oh jolly good, and yes! We have a cracking-good spa. We'll cater to your every whim and requirement."

He motioned toward the office, "Once you check in, we'll have a car waiting for you to take you two to the bank. Will you be dining in the room tonight?" he asked with a wide monticuled eye, and a smile on his lips.

"Oh yes, Morrice," Becky beamed, "you read my mind," as they walked off.

Chapter 14

The Freeport Yacht Club headquarters was an ultra-modern structure resembling a crescent moon. It laid east to west on Grand Bahama Island with the open curve of the building facing the north side of the island. At the center of the crescent was Morrice's office located at the east of the lobby area. The interior walls of the clubhouse where a brilliant white complimenting the sand of the manicured beach, which composed one quarter of the waterfront club. The exterior walls were floor to ceiling glass. It captured the island's beauty with the Caribbean blue water with soft fluffy clouds drifting above the tranquil bay. The outside temperature was a warm 80 degrees F with a gentle breeze that lessened the heat. The view of the wooden wharfs jutting out into the water, pelicans perched atop the pilings, hoping a successful fisherman would share their catch, composed the other three-quarters of the club. The panoramic view painted a fantastic picture for any water person, where millions of dollars of pleasure craft in every type lay moored. This was the elite side of the island. The view was very different from that of the bustling, working dock area of the city, where island steamers were tied up, offloading their cargos from, and destined to go to other islands around the Caribbean.

Morrice led the way to his office, after he whispered instructions to an assistant to secure KIS's plane. Once there, Morrice seated Becky and KIS in deep leather chairs in front of his marble desk.

"Mr. And Mrs. Swoboda," he started, "I need to explain that the 5,000 dollars you extended to us over the telephone was only the registration fee. I need to clarify that issue, first off. The yearly membership dues for the club and spa are $

25,000 yearly, of which the registration fee would be applied. I need the other $ 20,000 now please." He closely eyed the seated couple to see if they were of common ilk. The two nodded at each other and looked back at him unruffled by his statement. Seeing they hadn't raised an eyebrow he smiled, "I can leave you two alone, to discuss transfer of funds if you'd like?"

Becky nodded and smiled. Morrice stood and walked out the door leaving them to talk. When they were alone Becky turned to KIS, "What do you think?"

"Sounds fine with me, sweets, but you're the expert here. We can pay this guy in cash, if you think he won't betray us, knowing we are carrying money in the suitcases," KIS looked at her. "I'll go with instincts. I didn't bring a gun to protect us. I really feel naked without some kind of weapon. We're in your urban jungle. If you need them killed, I'm your man, but when it comes to schmoozin 'em, I don't have a clue," he winked.

Becky smiled, but also thought for a minute, "Let's pay him in cash now, the $ 20,000, and I want to give him a $ 10,000 tip. Morrice is a businessman. He's clearly helped us. I've had experience with people like him before. I'm familiar with this kind of situation. He can be discreet, but there's a price for his services. As long as we can pay, things are ok," she explained.

KIS flipped open one of the suitcases and Becky carefully recounted the bills. "This will make it easy," Becky said, "Three packs of $ 10,000. KIS, go and look outside the door. Nod to Morrice, so we can finish our business here."

KIS went to the door and saw Morrice standing against the opposite wall, at a polite distance. "We're ready," KIS told him.

Morrice recognized the piles on his desk. There was no need to count the money. People at this level trust each other. He'll count it later. If it were short, it could jeopardize their future business relationship. Morrice looked at Becky, "But you've paid me too much, Madame."

Becky shook her head, "No, Morrice. You've been a wonderful friend. The extra is a token of our appreciation. If you don't mind, we'd like to go see Herr Henkle now please. I trust your car will take us to the bank safely?"

Morrice leaned forward, "Madame, I appreciate your generosity deeply, and look forward to serving you both for many years to come. Yes, the car will take you to the bank safely. You have my promise."

Becky and KIS shook hands with Morrice, who escorted them to the waiting limousine. "To the Swiss bank, Thomas," Morrice instructed the driver as he carefully closed the door.

The trip from the clubhouse to the bank didn't take long. The modern white Rols Royse moved efficiently through the unusually colored buildings lining either side of the narrow street. Becky tried to roll down the window, but couldn't.

Looking through his rearview window the chauffeur explained, "This car is bullet proof, Madame. The windows don't come down. Would you like me to give you some fresh air?"

"Yes, please," she answered. "I'm having a little trouble breathing from all the excitement." She didn't want to let on that she was nervous and wanted to appear calm. She didn't want to worry KIS, who appeared calm at the moment, but who was watching her closely, for signs of danger, from her behavior.

Becky was on pins and needles until they arrived in front of the bank. The driver parked the limo in front of an impressive structure that announced to the world, wealth and position. A doorman from the bank in a white uniform opened the limo door and escorted Becky and KIS inside. Becky knew they were safe, now that they had made it inside this bastion. She had prior dealings with the Swiss banking community before.

They were very professional, very discreet, and very protective of their clients.

Waiting for them was a tall, blonde hostess in a crisp white shirt, dark skirt, black high heels, and carrying a notebook, who greeted them at the door. "How may I be of service to you today?" she asked with a slight European accent.

"We have an appointment with Herr Henkle, at noon. We may be a little early," Becky answered.

"Right this way," she motioned. Herr Henkle is anxious to meet you."

They walked through the marble building as their footsteps echoed against the walls of the gleaming stone structure. The building was as strong as the bank's reputation, solid as a rock.

The hostess opened a large heavily carved mahogany door. A man in his 40s with a dark tan, white hair, and mustache sat behind a huge desk. He was dressed in an immaculate white double-breasted three-buttoned business suit and immediately stood extending his hand to them. "Herr und Frau Swoboda?"

Becky took KIS's arm and guided him over to the desk, "Herr Henkle? Your reputation proceeds you."

After the initial pleasantries, Herr Henkle made them comfortable. Becky spied what she was looking for, a table to the right of Herr Henkle's desk, "Put the bags on the table, darling," she pointed out to KIS, "and open them for Herr Henkle please."

KIS walked over to the table, laid the suitcases down and lifted the lids, to display the contents. Herr Henkle walked over and looked inside the dark brown leather valises. He smiled broadly as his eyes subtly widened for a brief moment, "I see this is the beginning of a wonderful relationship. Please call me Siegfried."

Becky coyly smiled at KIS, lifting her eyebrow, as much to say, "We're in!"

All of this was new to KIS, so very different from his world. Becky, on the other hand, seemed right at home here, like she'd done this a thousand times. KIS deferred to her judgment. They made quite a team he felt.

Siegfried said gently, "I need to call in some associates, to help me with this large a deposit. May I get you some refreshments?"

Becky had been to hundreds of banks throughout the world. There was a protocol followed, a code subscribed.

"Yes, please," she answered, "we're famished. I'd like roast beef au jus, crisp string beans, mashed potatoes with ice tea, sugar and lemon please. My husband will have," she looked at him, "boiled lobster, garden salad for us both of course, Thousand Islands dressing on each, but he'd like an appetizer of jumbo shrimp with HOT cocktail sauce. Iced tea also?" she asked him, "sugar and lemon?" 'Wow, this is pretty special. Sure beats MREs,' he thought. "Sounds perfect," he answered her.

Siegfried nodded to the hostess who had been standing behind Becky and KIS, as Becky knew she would. A beautiful table with a crisp white cotton tablecloth, and a crystal vase with fresh flowers sat on the left side of Siegfried's desk, away from the money activity. Siegfried could coordinate people counting the money and attend to any questions or needs his new client's might have, as they refreshed themselves.

KIS leaned forward and whispered to Becky, "Wow, this is great. I could get used to this fast."

Becky winked over the intimate table, "That's my plan, darling. This arena is what I'm used to, what I was born to do. I just choose to do it differently than my mother. Her life was so cold, so unloving. All of this was like bloody combat to her. For me, this is an exciting game, to be enjoyed."

Becky motioned for Siegfried, "We have some legal matters to attend to. Do you have a lawyer on the premises?

"Yes we do, Frau," Siegfried answered. "I'll have him join you shortly."

Instantly, a cup and chair were placed at their table. It's refreshing to do business this way,' Becky felt.

The attorney arrived within minutes. Herr Weiss, a small man with large glasses and thinning brown hair, joined she and KIS, as they discussed some future ideas Becky had. After their wishes were outlined, Becky also discussed with KIS the possibility of dual citizenship. Herr Weiss outlined the pros and cons of the idea. They decided to proceed on that front.

There was also the point of establishing a business in the Bahamas, a base of operations from where their monetary transfers could originate. There was a friendly climate for tax-free financial accumulation here where business ingenuity was accepted within civilized limits.

Next, Becky wasn't sure what to do with her life, and so she wanted a legal opinion. "Herr Weiss, I am really eighteen years old. I have a Florida driver's license saying I'm older, that was, so I could get a job, the source of the ID we won't want to go into. I ran away from home earlier this year, from a domineering mother, who will stop at nothing to learn my whereabouts. I don't wish contact with her at all. I'm sure she and I will meet in the future, but when that happens, I'll be prepared. Right now, I want to live my life in peace. I ran away so I could live my life the way I want, with my new husband, without my mother's interference."

Herr Weiss was writing all this down. He and his associates would be busy, he could see. He estimated his fee for these services and his heart skipped a beat. Becky didn't bat an eyelash. She was used to these kinds of numbers.

"I have taken the name, Becky Wolefski, but wish to be legally married to Kyle. We want the wedding ceremony to occur in Florida. The ceremony," she looked at KIS, "is largely a celebration, but the legal issues and the possible harm a full wedding in Florida could bring to our friends there, worries me."

Herr Weiss sat back offering, "The legal marriage could be performed at our office, along with the straightening out of your passports, legal documents and such within two days. Can you stay on the island for that time to conclude your legal business?"

Becky looked into KIS's eyes, both nodded. KIS turned to Herr Weiss, "Can we be married this afternoon? At your office?"

Herr Weiss consulted his wallet calendar, "Yes, I can arrange that, and after we could have tea, say 4 pm?"

Becky grinned, feeling like a ton of bricks were off her chest, "Tea would be lovely," she looked at KIS. "Sounds fine with me," he smiled back.

Herr Weiss, of Weiss & Weiss, Attorney's at Law, had his instructions. He got up and extended his hand to each of them and said, "Everything will be done as per your instructions. You may be assured." He took his notes and nodded to Siegfried leaving the office.

Siegfried saw that they had finished and said, "Please bring your coffees with you back to my desk, and we can conclude the deposit. It is a sizeable one, I'm pleased to say. I count $ 1,970,000 dollars."

Becky nodded, "That's what I came up with also. It's to be a joint account, but would require both our signatures to withdraw more than 25% of the account," she looked at KIS, who nodded his agreement.

Becky walked over to the familiar suitcase and took out one pack of bills then walked back to KIS, "I want to take $ 10,000 for walking around money, so the deposit will be $ 1,960,000. By my calculations, considering the last international interest rate I knew about, we'll still be earning about $ 5,000 a day in interest?"

Siegfried walked over to a calculator on the desk then

looked up, "I estimate $ 5,324 dollars and 76 cents per day at current interest rate to be exact."

Siegfried handed Becky and KIS both a slip of paper, "This is your account number. Transactions can be referenced against that number." He also presented them with a checkbook, and new credit cards for each of them. "Is there anything else I can do to be of service to you today?"

Becky looked at KIS, "I'm not really that tired, are you?" she asked. Smiling, she looked at KIS and then back to Siegfried, "I want to do some shopping. I have nothing to wear!" she complained.

KIS grinned then nodded. Sleep could come later he knew. Becky looked at Siegfried, "Can we have a car and driver for this afternoon please? I want to look for a wedding dress, clothing in general for myself and my husband, and do you know of a good tobacconist you might recommend?"

"But of course, Frau Swoboda," Siegfried said, also looking at the hostess standing behind Becky. "All of this, the car and driver will be at the bank's door by the time you are there. Siegfried held out his hand, "Marie, my assistant can help coordinate your afternoon. May I say, what a pleasure it was to meet you both and to welcome you into our bank. Please consider us an extension of your family. We are here to help in whatever way we can."

Becky grinned, "We hope to make more deposits in the future, maybe not this large, but one never knows."

Siegfried shook hands and Marie the hostess escorted them out. In the lobby of the bank Becky stopped, "Marie, a moment please."

Marie nodded and stood patiently. She was at their service.

Becky guided KIS over to a soft leather couch, in a secluded alcove, and looked at KIS, "Is this ok with you?"

KIS shrugged, "All of this is so strange to me. I'm just a

farm boy on his first trip to the big city. I'm not used to all this fancy doings to be honest."

"I don't want to step on your toes or insult your masculinity by taking control. That's not how I want our relationship to develop," Becky explained.

KIS took Becky's tiny hand in his, "I don't feel threatened by you taking the lead here. Really, I'm overwhelmed. I'm just an ex-Marine Sergeant. These numbers are out of my ballpark. Did I understand we'll be making $ 5,000 dollars a day in interest?"

Becky grinned widely, "Yup. Our money will start to add up quickly. You'll get used to our new life fast. I do have an idea how to arrange things. I know you like things simple, and I'll honor that, but at times, I like to go shopping and splurge." She looked over at Marie, "Do you mind if I talk to Marie and set up our agenda for this afternoon? I know we need to be at Herr Weiss's office by 4 pm for our civil wedding ceremony, but we have several hours between now and then. I need to get some things. A girl just *has to* have some essentials. I don't even have any makeup! I fell into the Glades with nothing but my high heels, and I don't even have those now," she winked, "and tonight is our formal wedding night. I want to look special for you."

KIS leaned down and kissed Becky tenderly, "Go talk to Marie. I trust you hon. What is life between a married couple, if there's no trust?"

Becky grinned excitedly, gave KIS one more smooch, and bounced off to talk to Marie. KIS watched his woman play. It was beautiful and fun to watch her enjoying herself from a short distance away.

Becky talked to Marie, setting up their shopping for the afternoon. Then Becky walked over to the teller window and changed some of the 100-dollar bills into different currency and denominations.

Becky came back to KIS and handed him a small wad

of bills. "Here's some pocket change, some in US and some Bahamian money. We don't know what we'll need just yet."

KIS took the bills from Becky, who led the way to the bank door. She stopped long enough to give Marie a two hundred dollar tip, "Thanks for all your help, Marie."

Marie curtsied, "Danka, Frau Svoboda. You're most kind. I hope you have fun this afternoon. The International Bazaar in Freeport is a wonderful place to shop. Please keep the car and chauffeur as long as you like. The car will stay with you as you go. The police know our license plate and won't bother you. Herr Swoboda can use the car to sit in if he gets tired, or if you need a private moment. Some of the shops are small and might not have a seating area for your man."

Their car and chauffeur were waiting at the door of the bank, when KIS and Becky approached. Marie had telephoned the chauffeur their shopping stops via mobile phone while Becky was exchanging the money.

The chauffeur held the door open for Beck and KIS to get in. Becky leaned forward, "Can we go to the tobacconist first?"

"Yes Madame. My instructions are to take you to The Humidor, a fine purveyor of tobacco in all forms since 1754. It's only a short ride from here."

Becky leaned back and snuggled against her man. 'Oh, this is heaven,' she thought as she watched the brilliantly colored storefronts lining the street. The driver took them to the International Bazaar, and then turned down one of the side streets into the exclusive shopping area, where only the rich ventured.

The chauffeur stopped in front of The Humidor, got out and helped the couple step out. The minute KIS and Becky walked into the shop, their senses were bathed in the rich mingled smells of various aged tobaccos. Becky watched KIS's eyes light up with excitement.

"Yes, may I help you Sir, a tall European assistant, with

black hair, graying at the temples, bushy eyebrows of a scholar, in a bright white shirt, dark trousers and polished black shoes addressed KIS.

Becky nudged KIS, "Tell him what you are looking for darling."

KIS blinked, "I usually smoke Ashten cigars. Do you carry that brand?"

"Oh but of course, Sir!" I see you like the plain full tobacco taste, but of the mild Dominican blend. Do you prefer a natural or maduro wrapper?"

KIS was on familiar ground now, "I prefer a Connecticut-shade wrapper. I don't like the cigar I smoke to be overpowering, too strong. Do you have the corona and 8-9-8 styles? How about a robusto in Ashten also for a short smoke?

The salesman smiled, "Yes, we carry the usual shapes, but Ashten makes a short robusto for us."

Becky urged, get a box of whatever you need darling, so we'll have what you want. I want you to be comfortable."

KIS looked at Becky, a little unsteady, "These are expensive cigars. I'm used to buying a box a month, not three boxes at one time. I'm not used to spending this kind of money on myself."

Becky softened, understanding his hesitancy now, "Buy what you want honey. You're worth every penny to me. I want you happy."

KIS looked at the salesman, "I'll take a box of each. I need a new end punch, a good butane lighter, and a brown leather cigar case too please."

"Right you are, Sir. It is a pleasure serving a gentleman who enjoys a wonderful cigar. And by the by, in our humidity, you won't have to buy a separate humidor to keep your cigars fresh. Our climate is almost a perfect 70/70."

KIS looked at Becky, "That's 70 degrees Fahrenheit and 70% humidity. Just perfect for keeping a good cigar moist and fresh."

KIS asked, "I'd like an everyday walking around cigar, of a different taste, but still mild. Can you suggest something for me? Maybe in a bundle?"

The salesman paused, stepped behind the counter. He pulled out the end punch first and then presented KIS a tray containing a cigar labeled, Famous 2001, "Please Sir, take one of these and go out the back of the store, we have an open air veranda for our taste testing area. I think you'll like this cigar. It is smooth and cultured, a beautiful hand-made Dominican, if I may say so, Sir."

KIS took one of the 2001's and went outside, punched a hole in the closed end of the cigar and lit it. After only a few puffs, he'd enjoyed this cigar greatly.

Back inside the store, KIS said, "I'll have two bundles of those cigars as well."

Becky put their new credit card on the counter. She signed the slip. KIS was stunned by the amount for cigars, over 600 for the lot, but Becky didn't blink at all. She evidently was used to expensive shopping sprees.

Back outside in the limousine, Becky asked excitedly, "Where to next?"

KIS leaned forward and in hushed tones, spoke to the driver. KIS selected the next stop.

"As you wish, Sir," the chauffeur answered.

"Whaa?" Becky looked questioningly at KIS.

"It's a surprise," he smiled as he leaned over and hugged his little woman.

It was only a moment until the limousine pulled up in front a storefront; with 'Lichthy Jewelry,' on the sign above the door.

KIS grinned, "You said you needed some Bling if we ever got the chance."

Becky didn't know what to expect, but she at least knew they needed wedding rings for this afternoon. KIS escorted her inside.

As the couple stepped through the door, a distinguished looking gentleman approached them, "How may I help you today?"

KIS answered without hesitation and with assertiveness that surprised Becky, "We are looking for an engagement ring, but we also need wedding rings. We're getting married later this afternoon." KIS looked at Becky, "What shape diamond do you want, love?"

"EMERALD CUT," she blurted out. She had been waiting all her life to say those words. This was like her dream come true.

The salesman smiled, "We have a nice selection of emerald cut diamonds. If I might say so, I think we have the best collection on the Island. What size were you both looking for?"

KIS again, without hesitation answered, "Oh, two or three carat? What size do you have in a perfect stone?"

"Now this man is talking my language," Cathy chirped in.

Becky's heart raced with excitement. She was so happy she thought she'd cry from joy.

KIS seated his princess at the counter. The salesman brought out a blue velvet cloth to place the stones on, "Is this ring for show or for walking around?"

"Everyday wear for now," KIS answered. "When we get situated, we'll need to get some really fancy, evening-wear jewelry for parties.

"May I suggest a 1.5 carat? More than that is dangerous. We have a lovely 1.43-carat diamond that is flawless. I do have a two carat, but it has a slight blemish," he offered.

KIS held out Becky's left hand. The jeweler placed the diamond on her ring finger and the stone was wonderfully huge, but not over powering on her petite finger.

"OHH," was all she could say. She was having trouble breathing.

KIS took this as a good sign. He didn't see fear on her face at least. "Should we get it?" he asked his princess.

KIS got down on his left knee, "Will you marry me, Becky? Will you honor me, to be my bride? I didn't ask you formally before. You are more than what I could've asked for in life. You're my dream come true. You are my Goddess."

Becky flung her arms around her Monster from the Black Lagoon, "YES" she squealed. "A thousand times, YES!"

KIS asked, "Do you like yellow or white gold for the engagement ring setting?"

Burying her face in his shoulder, "You choose. Surprise me."

KIS looked at the jeweler, "Can you make a white gold setting while we wait? Price isn't an object."

"Yes," was all the jeweler said. He called the goldsmith over.

KIS explained, "I want a four prong setting with wrap around white gold filament for support. Can you do this now while we see your wedding rings."

"Yes," the jeweler answered. He leaned over to whisper to KIS.

"That's ok. Can you call Herr Henkle at the Swiss bank for fund transfer?" KIS asked.

"Not a problem, Sir," the jeweler answered as he called the bank. In a moment, he returned smiling.

The jeweler fit Becky's finger and the gold smith set to work alongside them so Becky could see her engagement ring being built in front of her eyes. KIS knew that an engagement ring was important to a woman. It was a sign of his commitment to his betrothed. KIS was demonstrating his feelings toward her. The timeless diamond, was an outward symbol of his never-ending love for her.

The couple chose a matching set of silver-toned tungsten wedding rings with a bright polished finish on a yellow gold band running around the center of the rings. Becky was in ecstasy. This was THE afternoon a woman waits for.

In just a jiffy, Becky had her engagement ring on and their wedding rings boxed up. With smiles all around, they left the jewelry store and into the limo.

"I have to get a wedding night outfit," Becky told KIS as they neared the limousine.

"Marie suggested La Femme," the chauffeur explained, "its an upscale woman's lingerie and wedding boutique, Madame."

Becky asked, "You better break out some of those cigars Kyle, I might be inside for awhile. Which kind do you think you might like to have first?"

KIS was like a kid in a candy store, "I might take one of each."

Becky leaned forward to the driver, "Will you be able to park in front of this store, in case my husband gets tired? I want him comfortable, but close at hand if there are decisions to be made, where I need his opinion."

"Yes Madame," the chauffeur answered. "He can sit in the car."

KIS walked inside the lingerie shop, where Becky was in her own kind of candy store. The beautiful young woman behind the counter was eyeing KIS.

"Becky, you better watch your husband or that man-hunter back there looks like she will try to make a play for him," Cathy warned. "Tell her she can look, but she can't drive his car!"

Becky turned to KIS, "Why don't you go have a cigar Kyle. I want my outfit for tonight to be a surprise."

"Ok hon, I'll be in the limo or sitting on the bench seat along the street," KIS told. Take your time and enjoy yourself.

Becky started cruising the racks as the saleswoman approached, "May, I help you?" she asked.

"I'm looking for a wedding night outfit to get my husband's blood boiling," Becky explained, "something hot, but elegant?"

After two hours of searching, Becky chose a white see through lacy baby doll with open back and matching back-tie keyhole panty, with white high heels. "Wow," Cathy admitted, "you look steaming in that nightie, girl.

The chauffeur drove the couple through downtown Freeport to Herr Weiss's office. The wedding ceremony was pretty simple, as it was a civil ceremony. Since there weren't extensive prenuptial agreements, really all was required, was signing a statement that Kyle Ibsen and Rebecca Allyson, now both Swoboda, were legally married. A light tea was served to cap off the afternoon. Then it was a quick drive back to the Yacht Club.

After a refreshing nap and dinner in their room, Becky changed into her surprise.

"Oh," Kyle exhaled, "YOU'RE BEAUTIFUL. You are more than I could've asked for," as she fell into his arms.

"I feel the same about you, my love," she sighed.

Kyle carried her over to the light switch and then the room went dark. Becky giggled, "Ouu Kyle that tickles," and then, "Mmmmm."

The next few days were wonderful. Becky got her legal life back, she was legally on her own, she had money in the bank, and a legal husband. She felt like a new woman.

Chapter 15

Despite her better judgment, Becky and KIS flew back to the Glades in the Flaming Eagle. KIS circled their island several times to make sure; there weren't any surprise guests there. He landed, moored the Eagle where she'd been, and covered her with the canvas tarp, in case they needed her again someday.

They'd already called Wela and asked her to perform the wedding ceremony in the fishing village. The village was a small community of about ten palmetto roofs, Wela's store, the wharf along the river, and an open sided community center where the wedding would be held. A wedding to a village was a 'family' affair, a celebration of a new adventure in life, for all to enjoy.

KIS had placed a call to Myrtle Beach, South Carolina to a pilot he wanted to act as his best man. Becky decided to not ask any of her friends or Blanche to attend the wedding fearing for their safety. She didn't want the drug cartel to find out, she was still alive, and to begin their manhunt again. She was sure Cathy would be there, so she didn't feel alone. Both Becky and KIS decided to just stay at the fishing village only long enough to get married, then get out of Dodge. KIS had planned their secret getaway.

Becky had taken several days in Freeport to decide on a wedding gown, but she finally found the dress that seemed to call to her. KIS picked a tux, a traditional white one. Becky was pleased that their wedding day was finally here.

The two stayed overnight at the fishing village. The wedding ceremony was to be held the next day. In the morning Becky changed into her gown in Wela's house. KIS bunked out in the home of a single man in the village. He was changing into his tux when he heard footsteps behind him.

"You look mighty handsome, fella," a familiar sounding voice announced.

KIS recognized it instantly. It was a voice he'd never forget.

KIS slowly turned around, "Montana! Man, am I glad to see you again. Thanks so much for taking the time to come. It means a lot to me."

"KIS," Montana replied, "I owe you my life. If you ever need a favor, I'll stop the world to answer your call."

"I really appreciate that, Montana" KIS confessed.

"Snap to Marine, we have a wedding to attend. I have to be back to Base tomorrow. I fly out to Nevada. I'm transitioning into F-15s," he grinned.

"KIS, did you ever consider coming back into the military, or at least a government job? We could use men like you. You have a special 'gift', should we say?" Montana asked.

KIS looked at his friend in the eye, "I never want to say never, and you'll always be a great friend. I miss Owl a whole bunch, but I felt him here. I know he's around and I've had closure. I can leave the Glades now."

KIS turned around, "I have a new wife and a new life. I want to try the civilian world and see what that has to offer. I want to try to be a normal couple, to travel, and be the master of my own destiny. If you ever have a special need for my help, feel free to call. You have my number."

The two warriors walked together to the community hall to wait for KIS's bride. The organist finally began the processional.

This was the first time KIS had seen Becky's dress. It was stunning. The dress was brilliant white and strapless, featuring embroidery and beading on the bodice, with a dropped waist, covered buttons and beaded embellishments down the back of the A-line skirt to the chapel length train.

Wela officiated at their wedding ceremony, which was a

combination of Indian celebration and event of passage. It was wonderfully different.

"Friends," Wela began, "we are gathered together in the presence of the Great Spirit combined with Mother Earth. We celebrate the joining forever of Kyle and Becky in the sacred bonds of togetherness. We wish them good health, wealth, and prosperity in all things. Is there anyone here who would object to them joining?"

Wela looked around the room. No objector was present, even Pima stood silent, allowing the ceremony to proceed.

Kyle we need your ring, to be placed on the finger of your woman, as tangible proof of your bond and her commitment to you throughout life. And Becky, do you have a ring, to be placed on the finger of your man, so that he would show to all, that all his heart and spirit already belong to you?"

Wela held the two rings, blessed them with sunlight, washed them in the salt and fresh waters of the Glades, and air-dried them in the four winds. Wela, the Mother of the Tribe, placed the rings on the fingers of KIS and Becky, "Neither of you will be allowed to remove the rings without my permission. It is our custom and our law." Then Wela placed Kyle's hand over Becky's, "You may now kiss the bride," she told Kyle. Their kiss was tender, but passionate. It was the beginning of their new life together.

The couple didn't stay long. Becky wasn't really into the tribe's usual diet, but she enjoyed the warmth of the villagers. Soon, they wanted to get going.

It was getting hot in Florida so Becky chose a bright yellow tube top and white short shorts for travel, with brown flat sandals. KIS wanted to show her something, and he ran with her to a dilapidated garage, something like one would see in the 1950s, made of cinder blocks and a slant tarpaper roof.

He carefully opened the double doors, and inside was a lump covered by a, what else, a green canvas tarp. "I might've known," Becky laughed, but she stopped laughing when KIS pulled off the tarp. "Wow! She's a beauty. Does she still run?" Becky asked.

KIS squeezed himself between the car and the garage wall; slid through the driver's side door and turned the ignition. The rumble that emanated from the old building rivaled a stock car garage area as KIS carefully pulled the car out.

"What is it?" Becky asked, looking at the sky blue car with two white racing strips down the center.

KIS looked like a proud Papa, "She's a GTO with a four-speed, a 454 cubic inch engine, complete with cream color cloth, bench seats," he grinned. I decided when I finally got a girl; I didn't want us to sit, apart from each other, in bucket seats like many muscle cars have. So I chose a GTO."

"Works for me," she grinned. "Let's get started, we're wasting daylight."

The departure was quick. Pima showed up with his new girlfriend. Now that he had the tourist business, he could afford to get married. Wela introduced him to a girl from a neighboring village that'd been ogling him, since he was ten. The young girl kept a good secret, but Wela heard of this girl's feelings. The Glades has a small permanent population and secrets are hard to keep.

Out on the interstate, Becky started toying with KIS's ear and nuzzling his neck. KIS looked over at her and pulled into the next rest stop, carefully stopping the car.

"Girl, there's a time and place for everything," he told her. "I don't want to get us into an accident now."

Becky scampered into his lap cowgirl style, facing him, "I want a kiss," she said in a spoiled brat voice.

Now that the car was stopped, KIS gave her all of his attention. In time, she gasped for air.

"WOW, I'm gonna have to get my hair unfrizzed after that kiss, Kyle," she laughed. "You curl my toes when you kiss me."

Becky got serious for a minute, "Our life has been a

whirlwind and unconventional, since we've met. We certainly didn't follow the normal routine in our courtship, but it all ended the way it was supposed to. Is this the kind of life I'm to expect from you?" she asked.

"Yup," was all he said.

She rolled her eyes and put her head on his shoulder still sitting in his lap, she was either that small, or he was that tall to still reach the pedals. Kyle backed the blue beast up and put her in first gear, speed-shifting up to cruising speed.

Back down the road, coordinated events were happening simultaneously. Two women received letters by messenger, both with return address Weiss & Weiss, Attorneys at Law, Freeport Bahamas.

Blanche was at the bus station dinner, sitting in her usual chair behind the counter. She started dancing like she'd seen a cockroach; "OH Golly, I got it!" she half laughed, half cried. She went to the center of the bus station and saw a half outside and half inside florist shop, complete with the name, "Blanche's House of Flowers," on the glass front window.

Blanche never knew what happened to Becky, the daughter she never had. She had been infected with pelvic inflammatory disease early in life and wasn't able to have children of her own. Her disease came from being raped one night by a drunken Carlos, many years ago. Maria had her helping to nurse him back to life, soon after she had arrived in Miami. Carlos never married Blanche, but he knew what he'd done.

Blanche knew Becky was alive, but would NEVER say anything. She'd only told two people of her secret dream, of owning a flower shop, to Maria and Becky. For all intents and purposes, both women were dead, but whose memories would live in Blanche's heart, until she met her friends in the after life.

Wela opened her letter. "OHH," she gasped as she read. She'd been accepted into the Law program at State University, her tuition and all expenses being paid for by a generous trust fund from some Swiss bank in Freeport, Bahamas. Her dream had come true! Now she could take care of her people. That was all she cared about. The people of her village, were her family. She also wanted to protect Mother Everglades too.

Back up the road in a sky-blue GTO, Becky asked, "Kyle, where are we going?" She noticed a strange necklace around Kyle's neck, one, she'd never seen before. She pulled out the iridescent blue medallion on a chain that had strange Aztec-looking markings carved in a circle, around the glass-looking metal pendent. "Is this something new, Kyle?" she was curious. "The markings aren't of a language I know of. Where did you get it?" she asked.

Kyle touched the medallion, "This was Snowy's lucky charm, but he'd lost it in the Kuwait Desert the day before he was killed. I feel guilty. I hadn't given him back his charm after I found it in our last camp, but forgot it, and then he was killed."

Becky touched his arm, "I know you deeply cared for your men. Can you tell me about the pendent? I know it's hard for you, darling."

Kyle had a lump in his throat, and it was difficult to talk, tears welled up in his eyes, "I want to head out west and visit Snowy's parents in Colorado and give them his necklace. I've already visited Aggie and Cowtown's parents in Texas, to let them know their sons were brave and didn't suffer when they died. They were good Marines, the best in my book, they did their jobs when called upon," Kyle said as a tear rolled down his cheek. "I went back to the Glades to see Wela, but I missed Owl so much, I stayed. Maybe I was supposed to stay, or we'd never have met.

Becky kissed him softly on his hard cheek, "It's strange looking back over all the events that led up to our meeting. I agree we were destined to meet."

Kyle looked at her, "I think it was fate, or a higher force

that brought us together, and now I feel 'something' pushing me to see Snowy's folks."

Becky smiled and hugged him, "I'm glad you can talk to me about your thoughts. It makes me feel closer to you, to know what's in your heart and mind."

Kyle shrugged, "I hear there are old gold mines out there that aren't fully mined out. Maybe we can find a ranch, something big enough for me to put a runway on, so we can buy an airplane, and fly around when we want. I know some friends who can help us hook up to a new thing called the Internet so you can connect a computer and trade on the stock market like you said you wanted. I saw first hand that you're a genius with numbers. You're brilliant with money. I'm proud of you, Becky. What do you think? Is it ok with you that we go?"

Becky put her head on his broad shoulder, "Ok cowboy. Sounds good to me. I don't know what's in store for us around the next turn, but I'm where I want to be. As long as you hug and give me a gentle kiss every day, I'm yours, forever…"